THIS IS ME !

OH! AND THIS IS...

Virginia Frances Schwartz

NUTZ!

illustrated by Christina Leist

Tradewind Books

Vancouver • • London

Other books by Virginia Frances Schwartz

SEND ONE ANGEL DOWN
IF I JUST HAD TWO WINGS
MESSENGER
INITIATION
4 KIDS IN 5E
1 CRAZY YEAR
CROSSING TO FREEDOM

Released in the US in 2012

Publisher wishes to thank Alice Herbert and Tasha D'Cruz for their editorial help.

Library and Archives Canada Cataloguing in Publication

Schwartz, Virginia Frances
    Nutz! / Virginia Schwartz ; illustrated by Christina Leist.

ISBN 978-1-896580-87-6

    I. Leist, Christina II. Title.

PS8587.C5786N88 2011   jC813'.6   C2011-901038-0

Cataloguing and publication data available from the British Library.

BOOK DESIGN BY ELISA GUTIÉRREZ
The text of this book is set in MYRIAD TILT.
MATI, BUTTSKERVILLE, TOLLE ONE and TWO TURTLE DOVES were used for titles.

FSC
Mixed Sources
Cert no. SW-COC-001271
© 1996 FSC

10 9 8 7 6 5 4 3 2 1   Printed in Canada by Friesens Corp., Altona, Manitoba in June 2011, on FSG paper using vegetable-based inks.

The publisher thanks the Government of Canada and Canadian Heritage for their financial support through the Canada Council for the Arts, the Canada Book Fund and Livres Canada Books. The publisher also thanks the Government of the Province of British Columbia for the financial support it has given through the Book Publishing Tax Credit program and the British Columbia Arts Council.

Canada Council   Conseil des Arts
for the Arts   du Canada

BRITISH
COLUMBIA
ARTS COUNCIL

For my brother, Sinclair T, the real Tyler—VFS

To my feline inspiration over the years: Big Red,
Mausi, Kitty, Pepper and Suki—CL

contents

Chapter 1

The Rescue

"Ruff! Ruff! Ruff!"

Three big barks changed my life.

Bruno the Brute was on the hunt. We didn't call him the Brute for nothing. He was a monster of a boxer dog. Even the mailman was afraid of him. He would not walk down our side of the street because of that dog and always left our mail at Mrs. Chu's.

I covered Tyler's ears with my front paws to block the barking noise.

Too late. Tyler woke up.

I dove back down beside Tyler's feet.

"Bruno's cornered something, Amos!" he yelled, bolting out of bed and flinging the covers off.

I had been stretched out in my favourite spot on top of his feet, white belly up to the sky, deep in dreamland. Clouds of dim sum steamed above my head. I was creeping into a nest of mice in Cat Heaven, ready to crunch their tiny bones when me and my blubber went flying to the floor.

Tyler raced to the wide-open window. I dragged myself behind. I'd follow him anywhere. He's my best friend, though he's just eleven.

Down in the neighbour's yard, Bruno paced around the one tree left in our neighbourhood.

That dog has a reputation. I remember when the junkyard down the block borrowed Bruno because their old German shepherd guard dog, Motor Mouth, got a three-day bellyache from licking rusty cans. Bruno ended up getting a bonus bone for biting a robber on his behind. That's all Bruno cares about now—bones!

Bruno clawed at a hole in the tree. He stuck his big black nose inside like a bear after honey. Suddenly the Brute howled. I hate when he does that. The Persian hairs on my back stick straight up like electricity hit me. All my grey stripes shiver. Actually I'm not one hundred percent Persian. I'm just Persian on my mother's side. The rest of me is pure alley cat.

Not if a hundred mice awaited me would I plant a single paw in Bruno's yard. Only the brave would go anywhere near there. Maybe if our mother, Francesca, were home, she'd go.

So I pointed to the clock with my tail, reminding Tyler that he was way late for school. He ignored me. He does that sometimes. He rushed downstairs and out the door in bare feet and pyjamas. From my spot by the window, I saw Bruno leap in mid-air with his shark jaw wide open.

WOOF!

Bruno made a muffled sound like something being sucked down a vacuum cleaner. The chain-link fence rattled as Tyler climbed over.

"STOP that, Bruno!" Tyler demanded.

He planted his skinny long legs a few feet away from the dog. Bruno outweighed him big time. Bruno stood still but couldn't say one word. Something was stuffed between his rubbery lips.

Tyler pointed to the dirt. "Sit down, Bruno!"

Bruno plopped on his haunches, stretched out flat, and whined a baritone tune so loud I worried it'd shatter the cracked glass in our windows.

"Let go of it right now!" Tyler ordered him.

The Brute did not let go.

Tyler stepped up so close to the boxer, his bare toes touched the Brute's claws. I sucked in my breath. Nobody gets that close to Bruno. Not if they want to live a nice long life. But Tyler knew what to do. That boy has instincts. He tapped Bruno on his black nose. That was his soft spot. The rest of him, even his short stub of a tail, was pure beef.

Bruno's eyes rolled up into the top of his head. He pleaded. He begged. Big crocodile tears dripped down his face.

"Drop it NOW!" Tyler's teeth were clenched. "Or you know what will happen."

That was his last word. There would be no more bones from our house if the Brute didn't listen now.

Bruno gave Tyler his sorry big-eyed look and spat out a dark blob. Then he ran off in a swirl of tail and blubber, burrowing beneath an old shed.

Tyler knelt in the dirt, grabbed a newspaper and lifted the blob up. By the time our back door opened, I was in the kitchen waiting for Tyler.

He spread the newspaper on the floor. "It didn't move, and I couldn't leave it outside. Bruno will be back for it."

A creature half the size of Tyler's palm lay on the chipped linoleum floor. It was black as midnight, except for the drops of blood. Startled eyes poked out of a furry face. Tiny hairs on its skin stuck up like bean sprouts.

Tyler gasped. "A baby squirrel! It's been hurt. Let's hope it doesn't die of fright."

Tyler did his thing, the same trick he used when he first brought me home two years ago. All I'd known before then was the streets. How my heart pounded when he had picked me up! Now Tyler spread out his hands and gently, like a brush of wind, laid them over the squirrel's pumping heart.

The squirrel's eyes widened. They shone like glass, unblinking.

The tips of two front teeth gleamed, small as pencil points.

Minutes passed.

Twenty tiny claws uncurled. Just like lights dimming one by one, the squirrel's breath slowed, its eyes shut, and its black head plopped to one side. For the first time in history, another animal besides Amos was snoring on our kitchen floor.

The baby squirrel was a sound sleeper. I crept up close to study it. It looked too young to leave its nest. It was smaller than Tyler's baby finger, so small that a coffee mug could have been its whole apartment. Its hair was see-through, like the first grass that pops up in spring.

"I'd better operate while this baby is asleep," Tyler said.

He set out a bowl of warm water, paper towels, peroxide, gauze and a shoebox. I clenched my teeth.

"Take a deep breath, Amos," Tyler said. "This won't hurt you a bit."

I tried purring to quiet myself but I wasn't in the mood to meditate. So I covered one eye with my paw and watched with my other eye while Tyler bathed the squirrel's tail where all the dog drool was. Teeth marks cut clear through it. Then

THAT DOG HAS
A REPUTATION

TYLER KNOWS
WHAT TO DO

WHAT
is
THAT???

Tyler wrapped gauze around its spiky black tail. After the operation, Tyler put the creature inside the shoebox and spread a paper towel on top. You'd never know we had a squirrel in the house.

Then Tyler jumped into jeans and a sweatshirt and stuffed a muffin into his mouth.

"I'd better run to school, Amos. It's nine thirty already," he said between munches. "I'm way late...again!"

I shot my tail straight up with a curve at the end like a question mark.

"Be on the lookout, Amos. Make sure the squirrel doesn't escape. I'll tell Mum about it later. She's going to be in for a big surprise, isn't she?"

Tyler bent down so I could give him the Head Bonk. The tops of our heads smacked hard against each other.

I sat on the windowsill watching Tyler run down the street in his soccer sneakers. My heart rose in my furry chest. Tyler still hoped for an after-school soccer game even though he was late for school again. Between rescuing animals and getting detentions for lateness, that boy was so busy.

Out in the backyard, there was no sign of Bruno. It was a crisp spring morning, with a brisk wind rustling the bamboo out back. An aroma blew from across the Boulevard. There must be a hundred Chinese restaurants over there cooking dim sum chock-full of shrimp, carp and whitefish. Ever since Mrs. Chu brought home a steamed fish ball just for me, I've been a Chinese food addict. My belly grumbled, but my food bowl was empty. Tyler had forgotten to feed me.

I was left all alone in the house with something in the shoebox and nothing in my belly. But Francesca was due home from the night shift soon. She would feed me. I crossed my paws and sure hoped so.

Chapter 2

On the Lookout

Normally I do yoga in my free time. We cats are so flexible. We can stretch into pretzels and knots anytime. I can do a mean Downward Facing Dog stretch that I learned from watching Bruno. It's a great before-brunch stretch because it creates more space in your belly. But since there was no brunch today, I slipped into a deep yogic relaxation instead.

I catnapped and drifted way back. Before I lived here, I roamed alleyways, dined in stinky garbage cans and huddled underneath porches on freezing nights. Brrr! Now I creep only as far as our backyard to chew grass and watch birds land in the bamboo. The rest of the time I spread out on the sunny kitchen floor with a belly full of hot chicken livers and an earful of Francesca's lullabies.

The noon sun was streaming through the window when I woke. I lifted up the corner of the paper towel. The squirrel was still asleep. I couldn't tell if the creature was breathing. I stayed quiet. I was on the lookout.

A dump truck roared past, and some flatbed trucks set the house rattling just like bones. I peeked out the window. There aren't many houses left here on the edge of downtown. Some are boarded up, ready for demolition. The rest have bars over all the windows and doors, like jail cells. These old houses stick up like crooked teeth between warehouses, factories and car repair shops.

That's when I saw Francesca crossing the street. She's tiny, but her heavy feet don't match the rest of her. She was rushing home from her night shift at Good to Go, a twenty-four-hour convenience store on the Boulevard.

Francesca stomped down so hard when she came in, the floorboards tapped like false teeth. I worried this old rented house might collapse. Sometimes, when it's really quiet, I think I hear termites munching on the beams in the basement. But I don't dare investigate. It's dark down there.

"Amos, you're waiting for me. How sweet," she said. "I worked overtime at the store. They needed me."

I decided to tell her everything before Tyler got home. That way he wouldn't get into so much trouble. So I made Big Eyes at her and turned my head toward the shoebox. Francesca stretched. She petted my back then sat down to read the newspaper. I whacked my paws at her newspaper, but she kept on reading. I puckered my lips and let my two front teeth poke out, imitating a squirrel. Francesca yawned. She asked me what Tyler wanted for dinner. I sat on my backside, pawing the air and pointing to the shoebox. I even sang a Meow in High C—the Alert Call.

Francesca finally noticed me. "Stop hitting flies, Amos! That's a bad habit from when you lived in the alleyway."

KNOCK! KNOCK! KNOCK!

I lifted my head, on the alert, hoping it wasn't our landlord, Stinky Feet, a man who never changed his socks. If you smelled something rotten, like a thousand barrels of raw garlic, he was sure to be close by. He was always looking for his rent money. Francesca was always looking for it too. Neither of them had much luck finding it.

The two of us sat very still in the kitchen. We barely breathed. It was better to pretend we weren't home at all if Stinky Feet was at the door.

"Francesca!" a clear soprano voice sang. "Amos!"

I was up on all four paws to greet Mrs. Chu. Whenever our neighbour came, her arms were loaded with bulging shopping bags full of goodies, and her front jacket pocket was stuffed with all our mail. I wound around her ankles and sniffed deep breaths. Mrs. Chu was a helper at Huang's

Fish and Meat Market and the aroma of blood and guts floated around her bag like a cloud.

"Oh, Amos, you are such a flirt!" Mrs. Chu's voice was high-pitched and tinkled like bells ringing. "I know what you want."

She opened one plastic bag wide to tease me. My tabby head sank deep down into it.

"Halibut and chicken livers! Gizzards! Fresh today. Just for Amos."

My belly flipped cartwheels. Strange cries gurgled out of my throat. I prowled like a leopard, stalking Mrs. Chu.

Francesca gave me an odd look, as if she were measuring my belly.

She didn't pop the gizzards straight into a steaming pot as usual. She shoved the bags into the fridge while Mrs. Chu put our mail on the table. There was a letter from Stinky Feet. I could smell it, an aroma like a football player's armpits double-dipped in hot garlic sauce. Phew! Some bills too. But Francesca did not look at them. She ignored my head rubbing against her ankles, and even my tail pointing straight at the shoebox.

"That letter is from Stinky Feet!" Mrs. Chu said, holding her nose. "When the postman delivered the mail this morning, my poor little Chico ran under the bed and hid. It gave him an allergy attack. Poor baby!"

Last year, Tyler had rescued a lost dog from the Boulevard. It was so tiny I thought it had shrunk in the rain. But it never grew. It turned out to be a Chihuahua. No one ever claimed it, even though we posted notices on all the shop windows. Mrs. Chu adopted it and loves it like a child.

Francesca shrugged. "Good thing it's spring. Stinky Feet is so busy outside gardening, he always writes to us for the rent instead of coming in person."

"Oh, Francesca, your rent's overdue again. How will you ever get the money?" Mrs. Chu asked. "Stinky Feet's sure to come over if you don't pay up soon. He'll march right in here with those stinky boots and sour socks. Remember what happened at the end of last summer!"

I gave Francesca the Big Stare.

"Those cheesy toes! The smell of old cheese was in my nose for months afterward. We had to leave the windows open all winter," Francesca said.

Tyler had trained me to use a special meow to alert everyone if Stinky Feet showed up. That letter stank so bad! I sure didn't want to smell the nasty landlord up close.

I was so hungry...but the gizzards were in the fridge. I had to do something about it. I stood in the middle of the kitchen and scratched the floor, calling both women to attention. I looked straight at the shoebox. They kept on talking. Then I meowed in High C again—the Alert Call. But they kept on talking. So I banged my tail hard on the linoleum—the Big Thump. Ouch! The whole floor shook. Did I imagine it or were termites leaping in the air? I was speaking Tyler Talk. But nobody was listening.

Suddenly, the paper towel began to rise up.

"What's in that shoebox?" Mrs. Chu shrieked, backing away.

The paper towel danced back and forth. Tiny paws stretched out. A head popped up, then one glistening black eyeball.

Francesca jumped up, hands on her hips, and stared hard at me. It was that look that said my brother, Tyler, and I were both in big trouble. Then her feet thundered across the kitchen floor. The paper towel trembled. Francesca lifted it off and the squirrel peeked out. Mrs. Chu hid behind a chair and peered over the top. The squirrel dropped back down into the box.

"This house is a zoo!" screamed Mrs. Chu. "First you adopt that homeless Amos and make him fat. Now you've got a squirrel in the house!"

Francesca frowned. "Bet I know who brought this squirrel home."

Francesca looked right at me. I gave her the blank cat face: I know nothing; I see nothing; I am innocent. But Francesca didn't believe me.

"What will you do with that thing?" Mrs. Chu asked.

Francesca shrugged. "It will have to go. But I'll wait until Tyler comes home. He has a lot of explaining to do. Meanwhile, the poor thing's awake, so I'd better feed it."

That sounded like Francesca. Eat first. Talk later. She was the queen of the kitchen, always stuffing everybody. After she fed the squirrel, it was sure to be my turn for treats. My belly growled at the thought.

"Well," said Mrs. Chu. "I brought sardines and a fish ball for Amos."

"Okay, I'll try that along with some water."

Francesca laid down the food meant for me on a newspaper next to the shoebox. The squirrel's nose twitched. But it backed away into a corner of the box and curled into a ball. It didn't like what was on the menu.

"Look! It's been hurt. Maybe that's why it won't eat." Francesca bent down to study the squirrel. "Tyler wrapped gauze around its tail. I bet Bruno had something to do with this."

"Bruno? I just brought him all these bones to keep him quiet," Mrs. Chu said.

"There won't be any more bones for the Brute unless the squirrel lives." Francesca grabbed the bones and flung them into the freezer.

"But Bruno will be barking day and night without them! Besides, a squirrel can't stay in a house. It's a wild critter. Let it go, or else there'll be trouble."

Mrs. Chu turned around and left in a huff. There was trouble in the house already: I was starving. And Francesca just stood by the window looking for Tyler, tapping her foot hard.

"Where is that boy?" she wondered aloud.

I jumped up to the window beside her. The street was empty. No kids. No soccer games. Tyler must be in detention. Francesca looked out again and sighed. If only I could tell her Tyler would be really late coming home from school. But she didn't speak Tyler Talk, so the two of us did what we usually do at times like these. We catnapped, belly up on the couch, waiting for Tyler to come home. Only this time, we were not alone. There was a box between us. Francesca held on to it tightly. She kept sneaking peeks at the sleeping squirrel, and paid no attention to my belly rumbling like a bowling alley.

Francesca had forgotten to feed me, just like Tyler had.

Chapter 3

A Day without Gizzards

Only Tyler would know what to do now. He once spent summer vacation at a chicken farm. He told me all about it. Instead of farming, he learned to hypnotize chickens. He taught them to dance to music. As soon as the music played, those chickens danced until they got dizzy. Tyler won First Prize at the County Fairgrounds for his Dancing Dizzy Chicks that summer. After that, he was a changed boy. He was an animal tamer.

All that afternoon, I waited and waited. It wasn't until dusk when Tyler finally came home. Francesca was cooking dinner. My Big Bold Stare stopped him in his tracks. My left ear pointed straight to his mother. This told him he was in trouble. Big Trouble.

Francesca pointed to the box.

"Where have you been and where did that squirrel come from?" she asked.

"Detention...Bruno started it, and then..."

By the time Tyler was done with his explanation, Francesca was in tears. He had used the word "blood" thirteen times. That was the magic word. Francesca didn't like blood. Instead of fuming at Tyler for all he did wrong, she was now furious with the Brute. Tyler could wrap most people around his little finger and get anything he wanted. All except for that principal, of course.

Tyler and I peered underneath the paper towel and the squirrel stared back at us. Then Tyler began to speak in a high falsetto voice to Francesca using long, stretched out sentences. It meant only one thing; he was hypnotizing his mother to get something he badly wanted.

"The-squir-rel-needs-to-stay-here-in-the-shoe-box-a-while," he said. "It-must-not-move-very-much. That-cut-has-to-heal-or-the-poor-squir-rel-will-bleed-to-death."

Francesca's eyes grew very wide as she looked at the squirrel's tail. She shuddered when she heard the word "bleed." Finally, she pointed to the treats in the box. "It has to eat. Or it'll die. But it wouldn't touch this food."

What Tyler said next won my heart. "Amos can eat this stuff. Squirrels don't eat meat. They're vegetarians."

That's when I made my move. That fish ball had my name on it. I dipped my paw into the box like it was a fishbowl.

"Amos!" Francesca yelled. "You're on a diet. Don't you dare!"

Did she just raise her voice at me? I knitted my eyebrows together, turned my back to her and sulked. Why didn't Tyler stand up for me? Didn't he notice my whiskers drooping?

"It's still a baby," Tyler said. "It may not have eaten solid food yet. But it needs to drink water soon or it won't live. Everybody knows babies need to be fed with baby bottles."

Tyler disappeared in the bathroom. He returned holding an eyedropper. I moved up close to see what he had in mind.

"Let's try this," he said.

Tiny drops of warm water fell down and hit the box. Plop! An eyeball popped open. The baby stared at the wet spots and then looked right at Tyler. Tyler brought the dropper closer.

"Ready?" he whispered to the squirrel. "Open up!"

A drop landed on the squirrel's cheek. Its tongue flicked out and licked it dry.

"Trust me now?" Tyler asked. "Here's something to drink."

He lifted the dropper right above the squirrel's head. This time, when the drop fell, the squirrel opened its mouth wide. Bingo! The baby blinked its eyes, swallowed, and then looked up for more. Fifteen drops later, the squirrel had drunk

itself silly. It sank beneath the paper towel and did not stir.

"It's a start," said Tyler. "We-must-get-squir-rel-food. Nuts-and-ber-ries. Things-it-would-eat-out-side-in-the-wild."

Francesca's eyes glazed. "Alright. I'll shop tonight."

Tyler's blue eyes opened wide. He was so excited he spoke in his normal voice. "Can we keep it then, Mum?"

"Are you kidding, Tyler? We have enough mouths to feed in this house. Let's help this squirrel get well. Then out it goes. Really soon!"

She served dinner. My family ate. Now it was my turn. Tyler ran off to do his homework. Francesca poked around the cupboards and inside the fridge. She did not take out the sardines. Or the gizzards. Instead, she sat down and wrote a list. I jumped up on the table and looked over her shoulder while she wrote: Apples. Walnuts and almonds in the shell. Blueberries.

I stretched out and fell asleep by my cat bowl. When I woke up, it was dark. Some diet cat food called Fancy Feasties for Fat Beasties was in my bowl again. It smelled like bad breath. The label read NON-FAT RECYCLED FISH HEADS. ADD WATER

FOR A CAT TREAT DELIGHT. Barf! You can't fool me. I turned my nose up and scratched my rear feet at it like my relatives do in the kitty litter box.

It was almost midnight. Francesca had left for work at the store that never closes. Bet that's where she bought this cheap cat food. Upstairs, Tyler was snoring. Detentions sure are tiring.

Then I remembered. I wasn't alone.

I eyed the shoebox. One lonely old gym sock of Tyler's was inside. And Holy Catnip...that sock was squirming around!

I wondered how long it would take for that rodent to recover? Deep down, I had my suspicions. Babies steal hearts. I don't want it hanging around until it grows up and turns ugly.

I CAN'T WAIT THAT LONG.

All I could think of was food. Mice were nibbling at crumbs underneath the floorboards where I couldn't reach them and termites were munching on the wood in the basement. But I'd never go down there. There were too many shadows in that basement. You couldn't tell what was hiding in the dark.

I went upstairs and flopped on Tyler's bed, tunnelling beneath the comforter until I found Tyler's ice-cold toes. Tyler likes his toes warmed by my belly at night. So I smothered his feet with my thick fur.

It was the very first day since Tyler found me that I didn't get my chicken liver treat. Though I had waited by my bowl like a soldier at his post and twirled around Francesca's legs a million times before she left for work, Francesca did not deliver the liver. She had squirrels on her mind.

A day without treats is the longest day ever.

Chapter 4

On the Mend

The next morning, everyone woke up late. It was Saturday all day in our kitchen. The kitchen was an old room with layers of shiny red and white paint and a black-and-white checkered linoleum floor. Francesca says our kitchen is vintage. It looked the same as it did when it was first built in 1930, except for the peeling paint, cracks and falling plaster.

I tapped the landlord's letter with my tail just as Tyler walked past the kitchen table. That boy never misses a clue. He pinched his nose with one hand and snatched the letter with the other.

"RENT PAST DUE!" Tyler read aloud. "Not again, Mum! Why didn't you say something?"

Francesca sighed. "I'm working extra hours at Good to Go. We had too many bills, so I couldn't pay the rent last month."

Dark circles showed under her eyes. How many times had I seen her shuffling overdue bills? I watched her raise Tyler all by herself, with my help of course. If it weren't for Mrs. Chu, we'd all starve. We certainly couldn't afford another mouth munching at our table. (HINT: Look in the box!)

Francesca pointed to the grocery bags on the countertop. "Here's food for the squirrel. But don't even dream you can keep that animal like you did Amos. Our only job is to get this creature well again. Squirrels belong outside."

I lifted my nose and sniffed. Nothing yummy.

Tyler unloaded bags of nuts, seeds and fruit. Vegetarian stuff. Not proper food for a growing boy or a starving cat.

Inside the box, the squirrel stretched out its tiny frame. It wiggled its nose like a rabbit and widened its eyes like magnifying glasses focusing right on Tyler. It tried to climb out of the box, but kept slipping back in until it finally scrambled up and dropped over the side. Then it hopped over to Tyler, dragging its crooked tail behind.

It looked up and chirped.

"It's hungry," Tyler said, smiling. "Let's see what it likes to eat."

Tyler held out a sunflower seed and the squirrel reached for it, took it from Tyler's hand, and swallowed it whole.

"You have to crack it open first," Tyler said. "It's in a shell."

Tyler showed the squirrel how to crack open the shell. Then he handed it another seed. The squirrel split it in two, then munched. Next Tyler held out an apple slice. The squirrel smelled it. Then it settled back on its haunches and chomped away.

"Chew it good," Tyler ordered, "or you'll get a bellyache from eating too fast."

One bite. Two bites...ten bites...twenty-five bites. All the while, the squirrel kept its eyes on Tyler, waiting for him to say, "Enough." Soon its cheeks puffed up like small balloons. Tyler quickly said, "Swallow! Swallow!" And that little squirrel finally swallowed.

Afterward, as soon as the eyedropper of water appeared, it lifted its chin up and gulped down every drop.

Francesca gasped. "The baby does everything you say. It must think you're its mother. Wish everyone around here would listen to me like that!"

They both giggled over that one. Their eyes were full of squirrel. Nobody was paying any attention to Amos.

When Mrs. Chu showed up that afternoon, Bruno was howling and my belly was rumbling. I twirled around her ankles until I was dizzy. Was it the starvation diet or could I smell meat pies in her bag from the organic pie place? I meowed a deep, wild growl from the pit of my belly.

"Here are the goodies, Amos. I've brought minced lamb pie for you and bones for Bruno.

He's been barking too much. We need to calm him down."

Francesca opened the fridge. The pies went straight in with the bones. The rest of the fridge was empty except for the bags of fancy nuts and seeds. I could read the labels: MACADAMIA NUTS (HAWAII), ORGANIC BRAZIL NUTS (THE AMAZON RAINFOREST), SUNFLOWER SEEDS (PROVENCE).

"No bones for Bruno!" Francesca insisted. "He hurt that poor squirrel!"

"The squirrel will get stronger soon," said Mrs. Chu. "Then out it goes."

"But the squirrel is in danger! Its tail is crooked!" Tyler gasped. "It might fall off. A squirrel uses its tail as a blanket or even a parachute as it flies down from trees."

Francesca sighed. "That's a lot of things for a tail to do. But the squirrel can't stay here. What if we take it to an animal shelter?"

Tyler shook his head. "It's too young. It'll be scared. It's quiet in our house. Why-can't-it-stay-here-a-few-more-days?"

There it was again: Tyler's secret hypnotic weapon—that slow falsetto voice. His blue eyes opened wide. And Francesca's eyes began to glaze over like muddy water.

Mrs. Chu stared at the two of them and frowned. "I know you two. If you keep this squirrel, you'll spoil it. It'll wear diapers soon and get chubby just like Amos. Besides, what if Stinky Feet finds out? He hates pets. He only likes Amos because he thinks he eats mice."

Tyler rolled his eyes at me. Talk about spoiling. We had all seen Chico prancing down the street in a purple polar fleece vest. Don't I get a vote? Boot the squirrel out today! Otherwise we'll never get rid of it. It's a freeloader. We can't afford to keep it in nuts. I saw the price tags. Ever heard of pignolis, pistachios and macadamia nuts? Neither had I until they appeared in our fridge.

"Stinky Feet only shows up when the rent is overdue," Francesca said.

"The rent IS overdue!" Tyler and Mrs. Chu spoke at the same time.

"I'll pay the rent soon," Francesca said. "He won't find out if we keep the squirrel a few more days. Hear me, Tyler? Three days! That's it. Now let's see what chores you can do today."

Tyler winked twice at me.

From my spot at the windowsill, I saw the soccer buddies walking toward our house. So I sang Meow in Low E—Soccer Alert.

Tyler downed a glass of orange juice in one gulp, wiggled into his soccer sneakers and headed out. "Sorry, Mum. My friends are here. I'm off. I'll do my chores later."

The door slammed shut.

"Wasn't I just saying something about how a squirrel listens and does everything it is told? But a BOY! How does Tyler always know his buddies are here?"

"Don't keep that squirrel too long," Mrs. Chu warned on her way out. "You'd better hope Stinky Feet is too busy weeding and hoeing his garden. If he finds out about it, he'll kick you all out."

My mother and I were now alone in the kitchen with the squirrel. That's when I noticed something odd. Francesca was smiling at the squirrel. She handed it a blueberry. The creature sucked the berry out of her open hand like a vacuum cleaner. Then it crawled into her palm and sat down. Francesca lifted the baby squirrel up in the air until they were eyeball to eyeball.

I looked closely at them. Francesca had shiny black eyes and black hair just like the squirrel. They both had tiny noses. The two of them were locked in a circle of quiet. Cats know things. We are psychic. Here's what I know. It was love at first sight.

The squirrel's eyes grew big and shiny as marbles. That's when I remembered that Tyler's prize cat's eye marbles had been rolling away mysteriously. We couldn't find them anywhere. Either Francesca was in a trance or she was losing her marbles too.

Soon that squirrel will take over the entire house. Gone will be my peaceful Dead Cat naps on Tyler's toes. Gone will be my warm seat on Francesca's lap.

I crouched in a corner of the kitchen with my whiskers turned down and my furry face wrinkled like an old sourpuss. Something caught in my throat. I felt a hiss coming on. After the hiss, I spat. Then I hissed again so loud that my spit flew across the kitchen.

"What's that sound?" Francesca asked. "Are you eating your fleas again, Amos? I told you to stop that. Fleas are fatty."

How could I tell her I wasn't just a cat? Or even a pet. I was Tyler's BFF—Beastly Feline Friend. Tyler was mine, all mine before that squirrel came along. And so was Francesca. Perhaps Tyler had gone too far hypnotizing her.

This whole thing was very worrying. I couldn't get to my gizzards either. They were tucked away in the freezer instead of warming my belly. What on earth was next? I sure hoped the floor-boards would hold us up.

WE CATS **KNOW** THINGS... WE ARE PSYCHIC.

IT WAS **L♥VE** AT FIRST SIGHT!

Chapter 5

Missing

Monday began with a "Beep. Beep. Beep." After eighteen alarms, Tyler flew off the bed and scrambled around searching for his jeans. He couldn't find any jeans, so he rushed down to the kitchen in his underwear. I followed him down.

Francesca pointed to a laundry basket of clothes she had just finished drying. Tyler grabbed a pair of jeans from the top of the pile, stepped into them and rushed out the door.

"Eat something, Tyler," she said, handing him a piece of toast and a lunch bag.

"I can't be late again. My principal says I hold the record for the most late days in the sixth grade. Can you feed the squirrel, Mum?" he asked as he ran out the door.

I looked over at the box. The squirrel had burrowed deeper into the sock, upside down. Only the tip of its bushy tail stuck out.

"Wake up!" Francesca called to the sleeping squirrel. "Breakfast!"

I remembered how when I was a kitten, she used to wake me up with the aroma of slimy chicken gizzards boiling away. It seemed so long ago.

Francesca bent over the box and called again. "C'mon out now!"

There was no movement in the sock. The tail lay stiff. Francesca's forehead wrinkled. She knelt down, peeked into the sock and shrieked.

"Where's the squirrel? It's gone! And...it lost its tail!"

I nosed on over and looked inside the sock. It was empty except for a black tail and a blueberry. The squirrel had gone off without them.

"You were a hunter once, Amos," Francesca said. "Find the squirrel. I guess that tail was ready to fall off. Hope the poor thing's alright."

Where does one look for a tailless squirrel? Behind the curtains? Beneath the sagging couch? Under the bed with the dust balls? In the shadows behind the toilet? The squirrel was nowhere to be found.

I returned to the kitchen with a blank expression on my face. Then I stretched my mouth wide so my whiskers pointed down.

Francesca frowned. "Maybe it sneaked out the door when Tyler left."

Suddenly we heard barking. Shivers hopped like fleas from one grey stripe to another until all my fur stood straight up. Outside, Bruno paced the yard, barking so loudly I thought he would choke on his own spit. The mailman ran across the street and the Brute soon quieted down. The rodent was certainly not out there. My fur settled down.

Francesca banged around upstairs, searching through the bedrooms. She flung all the covers off Tyler's bed, completely wrecking my nap spot.

Hours later, the phone rang.

Francesca answered it. "Yes, this is Tyler's mother. Oh, I'm so happy...I mean, I'm really sorry to hear that Tyler was dancing in the aisles. The class was in an uproar? Well, I'm glad you caught it. It never had its breakfast...Oh yes, I usually feed my son, but...I never had a chance to feed the squirrel. It must be hungry. Tell Tyler to share his lunch with it."

Francesca hung up. "That principal has no sympathy for animals! Mystery solved, Amos. Both our boys are safe and sound at school. And having a good lunch too. Let's nap."

I hoped Tyler wasn't in bigger trouble than he usually got into. If he were here now, he'd hypnotize me and I'd feel just fine. I had to nibble on that dry cat food just to calm myself. It reminded me of cardboard: bland and crunchy. It was definitely non-fat. The food soon disappeared. Francesca napped the afternoon away with an empty sock in her hands instead of me.

WHAT *IS* THIS?!

IS TYLER IN **TROUBLE** AGAIN?

By the time Tyler came home, the sun had almost set. He was carrying a cage. Inside was the black squirrel. It crouched in a far corner of the cage, shivering. It looked even smaller without its tail.

"It doesn't pay to be at school on time," Tyler complained. "I got a detention anyway."

Francesca's foot tapped down hard, threatening to break the floorboards. "Why did you take the squirrel to school with you?"

"I didn't take it to school, Mum! It crawled into my warm jeans in the laundry basket. When I got to class, I felt it in my back pocket."

"Your teacher said you were dancing."

"I was only trying to shake the squirrel out. But it shot up underneath my shirt and tickled me. The whole class was laughing so loud, the principal rushed in."

"Didn't you tell him what happened?"

"He didn't believe me. He thought I was doing a Dizzy Chicks Dance. By then, the squirrel had slipped out, and the principal dragged me to the office. Later some kids noticed the squirrel in science class. It had sawed through ten pencils and a box of chalk. The class went wild. The teacher caught it and put it in that cage."

Francesca giggled. "I told the principal the squirrel was our baby, and all the things it liked to eat. He thinks I run a zoo."

"I have detentions all week thanks to that squirrel," Tyler said, frowning.

Tyler and I both gave Francesca the Big Stare. My big brother had been betrayed by a rodent. I could picture Tyler sitting in a cold, windowless basement in detention.

"You had quite an adventure, didn't you?" Francesca said to the squirrel. "You do pretty well without your tail too."

She opened the cage but the squirrel wouldn't come out. Then she laid out water in an eyedropper, slivered almonds and slices of orange. The squirrel's nose wrinkled and its eyes fixed on the treats. The little baby crept out of the cage, sat down on its haunches and soon got busy crunching almonds between its buckteeth like a beaver, and sawing the orange, eating it peel and all.

"Still hungry?" Tyler gasped. "All you had to eat today was my apple, Joanie's Nutella sandwich, Sean's popcorn and the custodian's trail mix."

By the time it sucked up all the water from the eyedropper, its eyes closed. Tyler lifted it up and patted its full belly. Its tiny claws clung to Tyler as he slipped the squirrel inside the sock.

Soon the sock heaved up and down. I heard snoring. When you see someone snoozing, it's contagious. It'd been a rough day. I lay flat on the floor beside the squirrel in Drowsy Cat pose with my eyes closed and my earflaps open.

"NO!" Francesca insisted. "Absolutely NOT!"

"It'll have a hard life outside without a tail. It'll be too slow," Tyler said. "How-about-one-more-week?"

There were some "no's" followed by thirteen "bloods."

Then Francesca whispered, "Let me think it over. If I can pay Stinky Feet soon, we will be able to keep this little creature a little longer. But, if he should find out now, when the rent is over-due...let's just hope it doesn't rain. If it does, Stinky Feet won't be able to work in his garden, and then he'll come right over here."

Tyler gulped down three hot dogs in one minute flat, then headed upstairs to do his homework. Meanwhile, Francesca put on her jacket and got ready early for Good to Go. She must be working part of the evening shift plus the night shift too, now. She'd be out all night. She gave the sleeping squirrel a goodbye tap. But before she said goodbye to me, she circled a tape measure around my belly and measured me.

"Way too wide for a waistline, Amos!"

After she left, I hopped up on the bathroom sink and looked in the mirror. It was true. My stripes were expanding. They were no longer geometrical. They were wavy. That made me look fat. If only I were black. Ever see a fat black cat? They always look trim. Maybe I should get a black polar fleece vest.

I sat awake in the dark. My thoughts were churning. My paws were drumming. My belly was bubbling. I knew exactly what I was suffering from: cat burn. I couldn't digest dry cat food. I burped all night long. Dry cat food didn't give me the sleepy feeling cats crave, that deep yogic relaxation after the hunt is over. I needed something hot and stinky in my belly to settle it down. Ever since that sneaky squirrel took up residence in my house, Francesca has completely forgotten to cook me my gizzards. Gizzards are the best substitute for wild food that I know of.

If a wounded squirrel can turn a house upside down, what will happen when it gets well? So far, it has either been asleep, in shock or on a trip to school. Before the squirrel takes over the whole house, Francesca and Tyler had better wake up. Maybe I should set the alarm clock!

chapter 6

Showdown

Another week passed. It was Saturday morning, the official day for sleeping late. And the squirrel was playing hide 'n' seek again. There was no sign of it in the sock or in the kitchen. Squirrels spend their entire lives in the same territory, unless threatened. We looked it up on Wikipedia. Their territory can be as small as a city backyard. Rodents don't roam far. I wondered where it was hiding now?

I bounced up the stairs, my belly rolling like a crate of Jell-O. I tiptoed into Tyler's bedroom. He was snoring. My eyes shifted around the room until I found what I was looking for: Tyler's blue jeans. They hung on a hook on the wall. The back pocket was stuffed full. A huge walnut and three pistachios peeked out. Something was making itself comfortable.

I made like the Sphinx underneath the pocket— two front paws flat down, chest puffed out like a cobra, head stiff, eyes unblinking. I waited just like that.

Hours later there was some wiggling inside the pocket. A head popped out. The missing white knight from Tyler's chess set fell to the floor. A black nose sniffed. We were eyeball to eyeball. In the squirrel's black eyes, I saw myself, the enemy, reflected. I was ten times bigger than it.

Then the performance began. First, I warmed my throat by humming. I had learned how to do this by watching the Nature Channel's I'M NOT YOUR MAMA! where llamas were not in a good mood. A warning hum begins low and rises to a high pitch. Usually, that's enough to scare anyone away.

The squirrel chirped back in B Flat. Its tone was polite at first, like asking a question, "Excuse me, but what do you want, sir?"

Then it chirped louder and faster in a staccato voice as if yelling, "What are you staring at?"

Finally I spat like an angry llama.

The squirrel spat back from between his buck-teeth. Nut breath! Luckily, I ducked.

My turn. This time, I hissed deep and long. This comes from my own training as a cat, although llamas do it too. My face turned sour lemon and my head furs rose up, making me look like a beastie cat on a bad hair day.

Here's what I told the squirrel: "Get out of that pocket NOW! Get out of this room! Tyler's room is MINE, all mine!"

That made an impression: it began to chatter loudly non-stop, jerking its whole body. Each paw, each claw, even the stump of its tail shook.

"I WON'T!" it announced. "You can't make me!"

The squirrel ground its teeth. It didn't jump down like I ordered it to.

That left me no choice. I had to behave like any cat would when their territory was threatened. I had to show it who was boss. So I flicked a walnut at it. The nut bounced off Tyler's jeans and dropped to the floor with a thud.

The squirrel and I had reached a stalemate, so I dove onto Tyler's feet. Two little love nibbles and then a good long scratchy lick with my sandpaper tongue. This made Tyler mine, all mine.

Tyler woke up. "Hey, isn't that cute?" he said, stretching. "The squirrel has made a nest in my old jeans."

Tyler began to chirp at the squirrel. The squirrel stared.

"How about you chirp once for yes and twice for no? Would you like some new nuts to eat right now?"

The squirrel was silent.

Tyler tried again and again, but he couldn't get the squirrel to say anything back. Obviously, the squirrel did not understand Tyler Talk like I did. Its head was as thick as a walnut. Come to think of it, it was shaped like one too.

I made a plan then and there: gather evidence; get even. Watch the squirrel every minute of every day. Sneak up on it in the dark.

While I was tiptoeing around a corner later that day, I caught it doing a Downward Facing Rodent pose. This is a yoga stretch where the body makes a V-shape with all four paws flat on the ground. The squirrel's backside shot way up in the air and its nose touched the floor. I could hear its teeth sharpening. It was turning into a Samurai warrior rodent.

HOW GRACEFUL!

SAMURAI WARRIOR RODENT!

How someone does yoga tells you a lot about them. Take me, for instance. My favourite move is Dead Cat pose with a lot of purring. This is where I lie flat on my back, belly up to the sky, with all four paws stretched wide. I don't move in this position. That's not because I'm really dead. I'm sound asleep. What that says about me is that I am mostly mellow on my Persian side, unless bothered by a squirrel. That's when I turn into an alley cat.

We had a routine come Saturday night, Francesca's night off. After dinner, we all brought snacks into the living room and spread out on the sofa to watch television.

Just before the big night, around dinnertime, things took a turn. My catnip mouse was missing. It was a raggedy pink mouse with a faded hint of catnip and I loved it like Tyler loves me. But before I could look for it, I got distracted by a stinky odour. Tyler was cutting bluefish from Carp Bay into bite-sized sushi just for me. No one dared eat those rotten fish. But I took my chances. It had a smell to die for.

It was time to play Catch the Sushi. Tyler held a slice of sushi at counter level. I jumped for it. Gotcha! Then he held the next piece up a few inches higher. We played until I couldn't reach it anymore. The highest I'd ever got was the top of the fridge, but that was when I was a lot younger and thinner. I swallowed the sushi whole as Tyler was always ready with the next piece in his fingers. No time to chew. I was known to growl like a lion during this game. That made Tyler laugh until his belly hurt.

Afterward, he carried my leftover sushi on a tray into the living room with his buttered popcorn, Francesca's potato chips and the squirrel's bag of shelled walnuts. We settled in for the evening. The television muttered. Tyler and his Mum munched. I crunched. The squirrel cracked.

Tyler is a hungry boy. When his gigantic bucket of popcorn and all Francesca's potato chips were gone, he threw the squirrel a shelled walnut. The squirrel dug its buckteeth right down the middle of the walnut and split it in two. Quick as a karate chop, Tyler whisked out his hand and stole the walnut halves out of the squirrel's paws.

The squirrel's head whizzed right, then left, searching for the nut. We all heard the whistles from the rodent when Tyler popped the nuts into his own mouth. Sounded like curses to me.

"Let's make a deal," Tyler told him. "I'll give you some nuts and you crack one for me. How about it?"

Tyler held up a huge walnut like a question mark. The squirrel eyed the nut and chattered furiously. I'd heard that kind of foul language before. The squirrel was giving Tyler an argument.

Tyler dropped the walnut back into the bag. "So you don't want to play Nutcracker."

"Stop teasing the little guy," Francesca told him.

Tyler pretended to watch television. The squirrel was totally silent. It stared at the nut bag and then at Tyler. Tyler and I watched the Nature Show WILD THINGS THAT MAKE YOU LOOK TAME. I fluffed my fur up like the lion on the show to make Tyler laugh. He petted my fur back down to normal. When the commercial came on, the squirrel chirped.

"Yes?" Tyler asked.

Two loud chirps. Two eyeballs on the nut bag.

"Is it a deal?" Tyler continued.

Two sweet chirps.

"Good. Here's your walnut." Tyler grinned. "I'll let you know when it's my turn."

Nuts got tossed one by one to the squirrel. Two minutes later, Tyler held up a supersized walnut. The squirrel stared straight at it.

"This one is for me, remember?"

He tossed it to the squirrel. The squirrel held on to it tightly like it was the last walnut in the world.

"Do we have a deal or not?"

Tyler pretended to crinkle the nut bag as if he were closing it forever.

The squirrel blinked. It swallowed. It looked at Francesca, hoping she'd save the day. But she just shrugged her shoulders as if to say, "It's between you two boys." The squirrel was cornered. It dug its buckteeth into the walnut and cracked it in two. Tyler opened his hands and held them out. The squirrel neatly placed one half of the walnut and then the other half into Tyler's palms.

I bet you could hear Tyler's laughter all the way to the Boulevard that night. It was the smartest trick Tyler had ever pulled off. Now an animal was feeding Tyler instead of the other way around. I had to sit there and listen to it all. I whacked my tail down hard—the Big Thump. We'd never get rid of that nut-cracking squirrel now. I was so disgusted I decided to go to bed early.

I bounced off the sofa and headed out of the room. But just before I left, something pink flashed and caught my eye. Underneath the sofa cushion my catnip mouse was neatly tucked between the layers of fabric. It hadn't just rolled there. Someone had hidden it. Let's just say I knew who that someone was.

Chapter 7

Return of the Bones

"You are in big trouble now,

Francesca!" Mrs. Chu said, rushing into our kitchen the next day, her soprano voice higher than usual. She carried a Huang Market bag with a strong fishy scent.

I was so hopeful, my whiskers smiled.

"I just passed by the Chinese takeout," she said, panting. "Mrs. Wang told me she noticed a squirrel hanging on your living room curtains."

Francesca frowned.

Mrs. Chu continued, "She told all the workers in the junkyard too. The news upset Motor Mouth. Can you hear him?"

High-pitched yelps cut the air. Bruno joined in, howling in his big baritone. My poor Persian hairs were electrified. I thought I heard the word "Bones!" in the Brute's conversation. That's all he talked about lately.

Mrs. Chu pointed to the junkyard. "Now he's set Bruno off. The whole street will wonder what's happening. Stinky Feet is sure to find out."

"Oh no!" Tyler shouted. "Stinky Feet owns the junkyard. If he knows about the squirrel, he'll make us move out."

The squirrel heard each and every word. It crept close to Tyler's feet. Suddenly it scooted up his legs, then whizzed across his belly, up his chest and settled on his shoulder.

Francesca gasped. "Look how it's perching on you. It wants to stay. But it just wore out its welcome."

"Let it out today," insisted Mrs. Chu. "It can take care of itself now."

"Alright." Francesca sighed. "One more day."

"One more day? Why wait?" Mrs. Chu continued. "Bruno's barking will give the whole neighbourhood a headache. Without his bones, he's a wild dog. Look at poor Amos. He's frowning. He must hate all the barking."

I looked up at the mention of my name.

"That's because I've put him on a diet," Francesca said. "His belly reaches to the floor and swings back and forth when he walks. He is put out now, but in the end, he will feel much better."

The three of them turned their heads and stared at me. Even the squirrel studied me with bright buggy eyes. I lifted my chin high and pretended not to see any of them.

"Nonsense!" Mrs. Chu said. "Amos loves to eat. He lives for it. I'll feed him this raw fish myself if you won't."

That was sweet music to my ears.

Mrs. Chu dropped the fish right into my bowl. I was soon in sushi heaven, grinding sweet smelt bones between my teeth. Good thing Mrs. Chu was on my side or I'd be skin and bones.

"If you're going to feed Amos, we may as well feed Motor Mouth too," Francesca said.

From its perch, the squirrel chirped low tunes into Tyler's ear. Tyler chirped back some. They were having their own conversation in Squirrel Talk. Bet that rodent was begging Tyler to stay.

Tyler smiled. "What a great idea! If we give Bruno's bones to Motor Mouth, at least there will be one less barking dog and the workers will be happier. And maybe we'll get to keep the squirrel longer."

Tyler petted the squirrel. "Poor baby. Lost your family. No name either."

My stripes quivered like there was a sudden draft. I had felt it coming. They both wanted to give the squirrel a name. When no one was around, I had heard Francesca practising squirrelly names out loud: Bucky, Claws, Fuzzball. Here's what I know. Pets get names. Cats, of course, and even dogs. Sons and daughters, maybe. But not a wild animal. Naming it meant only one thing—it'd be a keeper.

"How about Blue Jeans?" suggested Tyler. "Or Blue?"

Francesca sighed. "You'd better not name it. It'd be too hard to give it up. It'd be one of the family."

"Alright. Alright," Mrs. Chu said, cutting in. "I'll take Bruno's bones to Motor Mouth. But you need to come up with a plan for letting that squirrel go."

Francesca got busy slicing vegetables for a dinner of pasta primavera with dark red tomato sauce. I never touch the stuff, but Tyler could slurp a whole pot of pasta in five minutes. The vegetables were added to slow him down. He did not need a diet. He was built like a string bean.

Tyler sat down to talk with Mrs. Chu. Much to my dismay, the squirrel did not budge from its perch on his shoulder. I thought only birds like owls, pigeons or robins perched. My neck got a kink from looking up at the rodent.

"If I let the squirrel out, it-might-fall-from-the-oak-tree. Then-Bru-no will-get-it!" Tyler insisted in his falsetto voice. "Without a tail, it can't jump, bal-ance, right-it-self, or-ev-en-talk-to-oth-er-an-i-mals."

Mrs. Chu headed toward the door. She was wearing only one sock. "It has to go. Squirrels can't be trusted indoors."

Try as hard as he could, Tyler could not hypnotize Mrs. Chu. She must have chihuahua blood in her.

It was now the squirrel's turn for dinner. A squirrel's whole day is a twenty-four-hour buffet. Squirrels are vegetarians. Vegetarians are always munching and stashing food to eat later. Squirrels are fidgety and restless because all they eat are nuts. They have no focus. Nuts don't fill you up. Tiny nibbles of nuts will make you hyper.

Cats eat chicken gizzards or mice. Those foods calm you down and head you straight into the blissful slumber of Dead Cat pose. A bellyful of meat or fish means peace. Why else do you think we cats sleep sixteen hours out of twenty-four?

After dinner, while Francesca headed into the basement to do laundry, Tyler taught the squirrel a new game: Catch the Nut. He threw a huge Brazil nut up so high that it landed on top of the fridge. The squirrel flew into a flying trapeze act. First it leapt from the floor to the windowsill. Next it hopped to the top of the table before scrambling up the curtains. Finally it made a breath-holding jump, its little stump of a tail shooting out like a rudder, and grabbed the nut.

Tyler clapped at this performance. "You can survive without your tail after all. But...shhh!

Don't show Francesca or you'll be out the door."

Then Tyler grabbed his soccer ball and headed out the door, leaving me alone with you-know-who. Now was my chance to show off my talent for speaking other languages. I'm so good at learning languages that I figured out how to mimic a cricket chirp: ch-ch-ch-ch-ch! I use it to trick birds when they land in the bamboo looking for crickets to eat. When the birds get close, I whip my paw out at them. But so far they'd been too fast for me.

Maybe I could try talking like a squirrel. I hid behind the couch and chattered, a little husky at first. I lifted it up a few notes and revved up the speed. A click of the tongue at the back of my throat. Got it! Squirrel Talk. I practised until... claws clicked on the wood floor. I chirped once. The claws stopped. Then I let loose all the chatter I had heard during our fights. I repeated each and every staccato syllable.

The squirrel spit. Its stump of a tail flicked super-speed against the floor. I kept on chattering. The rodent went nuts. I had it good. From between its front teeth came high-pitched whistles. It raced all over in circles, flew up and landed on the couch, sinking its claws into the fabric.

Suddenly Francesca's feet thumped into the room. "What's going on in here?"

The squirrel's chirp was so high-pitched that my ears hurt.

"Stop this nonsense! Look what you've done to the couch!"

Through the open window, Bruno howled. The chain-link fence rattled as the boxer heaved his body against it.

"You'd better settle down or we'll put you back outside. And I'll have to tell Tyler about this too."

The squirrel gulped. A grin lit up my face like a light bulb. Cheshire, it's called. That's one big cat grin.

Afterward, Francesca sat down in the kitchen with her book and I joined her. She sighs a lot when she reads. I guess her books are sad. Maybe they're memoirs. Just as I began rubbing my back against her ankles to remind her I was hungry again, the squirrel ran past. Its face was dark and saucy and its breath stank of garlic. Bet it'd been eating pasta leftovers on the counter.

It hopped up and perched on Francesca's shoulder. They chattered back and forth. The two of them were wrapped up in a world of their own.

They didn't notice me under the table. Francesca was a double agent. She had pretended she wanted the rodent out. But now she'd gone over to the squirrel's side. She'd betrayed me.

I had no more hiss left in me. Or a spit.

Soon Francesca would leave for the night shift. Soon she'd have to pay the rent. Soon she'd have to put that creature out. But exactly when? That was the question that was giving me indigestion.

NUTS: - DON'T FILL YOU UP
- MAKE YOU HYPER

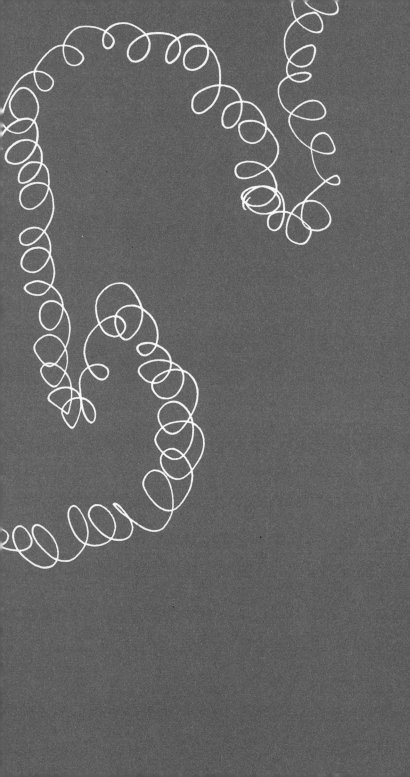

Chapter 8

Sounding the Alarm

Early the next morning,

the squirrel woke me up with its chattering. It poked out of the jean pocket with missing dice from the Monopoly game in its paws. Its face was strawberry red, matching the colour of the Jell-O in the kitchen, but its buckteeth blazed bone-white, blinding me like the flash of a camera.

I crept into the bathroom. The toothpaste was high up on the sink and it took ten leaps for me to get up there.

Whew! I made it.

Just like I figured. Teeth marks cut through the tube of toothpaste like train tracks. Toothpaste had leaked out everywhere.

Only one thing to do: snitch on the rodent.

I licked Tyler awake and gave him one of my Big Bold Stares, the one where I tilt both ears backward, meaning Follow Me.

Soon as Tyler saw the mess, he marched back into his bedroom and came back holding the squirrel. Then he set it down on the sink.

"Look at this mess! Toothpaste is not food!"

The rodent yawned, nibbled on the toothpaste tube and swallowed.

"NO!" Tyler yelled. "You can't eat it! Don't hop on the sink, ever!"

Just as I expected! He was having no luck training the squirrel. But I won't dare suggest that he hypnotize it. That's how he changed me from an alley cat into a house cat. I'm Tyler's success child. When he hypnotizes me, it gets very still. I hear everything, but it's as if I am floating in the air.

My first hypnosis lesson was really stinky. Tyler pressed a letter from Stinky Feet flat on my nose.

"ME-OO-OW!" I spoke up right away. Armpits and garlic. Phew!

"Good start. You need to rev it up. Remember when that car alarm wailed all night out on the street and kept us all awake?"

I nodded.

"You-must-make-that-sound, A-mos, A-mos... N-O-W!"

It took only two days of hypnosis for me to make a sound like a car alarm. By that time, Francesca was a nervous wreck. She kept checking outside to see whose car was making that racket. She never guessed it was me yelling the Stinky Feet Alarm: "YE-O-W! YE-O-W! YE-O-W!"

That afternoon the squirrel made more trouble. Give a squirrel some dirt and it will dig from here to Singapore. I caught the squirrel digging in the

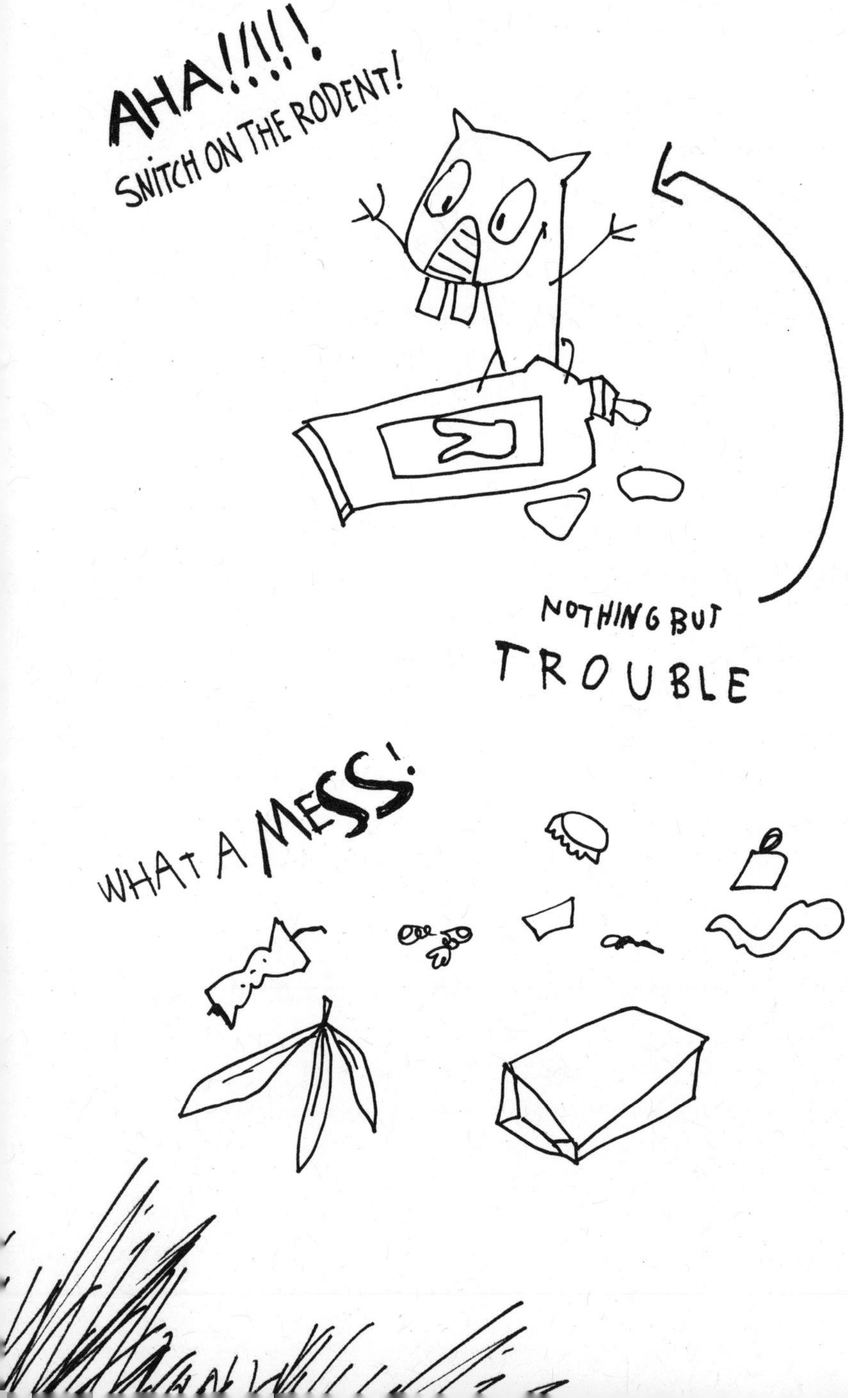
AHA!!!!!
SNITCH ON THE RODENT!
NOTHING BUT
TROUBLE
WHAT A MESS!

kitchen garbage can face down, stump up. Up flew carrot peels, coffee grounds, gooey plastic wrap, tomato sauce and a banana skin splattering the wall. Tomato sauce dripped down from the ceiling onto my head. When I meowed at all the mess, it scampered out of the kitchen and ran upstairs. That's when I investigated. Sure enough, one fat hazelnut was buried at the bottom of the garbage can underneath a soiled napkin.

Just at that moment, Francesca walked in. Coffee grounds sat on my whiskers and the ceiling was raining tomato sauce.

"Amos! Are you eating out of the garbage?" Francesca said, scolding me. "You are so jealous of the squirrel, you are doing very bad things for attention. This is alley cat behaviour!"

High-pitched staccato cackles echoed from upstairs. What could I do then but spend the rest of the day hiding in the dust balls behind the couch?

Hours later, I heard Tyler calling me. "Look, Amos! There's a newspaper contest for the funniest painting of a dog."

I refused to come out of my hiding place. I wasn't interested in other animals right now, especially dogs.

"Amos, come out. I have an idea."

My tail peeked out from behind the couch, lifting straight up with a curve at the end like a question mark.

"There's a big prize for this contest, enough money to pay the rent for two months or more."

I purred in agreement.

Tyler scrunched up his face. "But I can't draw at all. Besides, we don't have watercolours, paint or canvas and there's no money to buy any. Let's forget the whole idea."

Tyler began to sigh just like Francesca, loud as a bus wheezing to a stop. He was having no luck training the squirrel (good news!) and no idea how to help pay the rent (bad news!). After an early dinner, Francesca left for work and Tyler stretched out, yawning, on his bed.

Soon it began to rain, harder and harder. Wind rattled the windows. Lightning lit the rooms. Thunder shook the doors. I tried napping on the couch but could not sleep. The Brute began to howl louder and louder. Who was out there? Mailmen don't deliver at night. It was time to inspect. No one was in the backyard so I hopped up onto the front window in the living room. Out there, in the empty street, someone huddled in a big raincoat and umbrella. He stood very still, watching our house.

Just then, all thoughts stopped. My brain shut down. A cloud of stink fog blew through all the cracks in this termite-ridden house. My nose shrivelled up. It was garlic and armpits alright.

There was no doubt about it: Stinky Feet was outside.

I sounded the Stinky Feet Alarm: "YE-O-W! YE-O-W! YE-O-W!" over and over like a car alarm that got stuck—a cappella. All meow and no music.

Upstairs, I heard the thump. Tyler had jumped out of bed. In the next minute, he was right behind me. He pinched my nose first, then his own nose. We both peeked out the window.

"It's him alright," Tyler whispered. "He's heard about the squirrel."

Claws clicked on linoleum. The squirrel ran into the living room from the kitchen. Red flakes dotted its black face.

Tyler called to it. "C'mon up here and be still."

The rodent tried to hop onto Tyler's shoulder but I swatted my tail at it and it fell back. It slowly clawed its way up Tyler's pants and got to its perch anyway. There was a new smell. Something hot and peppery like the red-hot Cajun leftovers from dinner. That's what was all over the squirrel's face! I sneezed. Out in the street, Stinky Feet suddenly turned our way.

"Get down!" Tyler warned us.

A minute later, we peeked out the front window again. Stinky Feet was no longer there. Suddenly shivers hopped up my spine. An odd odour, like mouldy armpits that had not been washed for years, filled the living room. The squirrel's nose quivered faster than a hummingbird's wings.

That's when I saw it.

A soggy letter was sliding underneath the front door. I made like a statue, pointing my tail straight at it. Tyler crept toward the letter. The squirrel and I backed away.

"It's from Stinky Feet!" Tyler gasped. "'Second notice! No rent! If I do not get the rent soon, you are out on the street!' We have to do something soon, Amos!"

Tyler gave me the Big Stare. Winter was coming. We couldn't even stay in the bamboo since it belonged to Stinky Feet too. There'd be nowhere to go and nothing to eat outside. That was how my life began, in the alleyway. I couldn't go back there. I had to do something.

It was now or never.

Brute
howling

STINKY FEET
APPROACHING!!!!!!

THE
DREADED
LETTER

Chapter 9

Colour Me Blue (and Red)

The next day I stood at the top of the basement stairs. If I don't do it now, I told myself, we have no chance to pay the rent. I had to be brave for Francesca and Tyler. Besides, if we got kicked out of the house I would have nothing to eat. So I had no choice really. I had to go down and investigate.

I'd only been down there once. Lots of spider webs and odd sounds. But I remember shelves of stuff Stinky Feet left. Bet there was paint down there. Tyler could use it for the contest.

First I did a Downward Dog stretch to loosen up. Then I breathed a deep yogic breath, filling my lungs with courage and strength, and fluffed up my chest like a lion in case I met an enemy. One paw, then the next, slowly I crept down into the darkness below.

There was no mistake about it. There was definitely crunching in the basement. A musty odour. And wheezing. Or was that a cough? I wasn't sure I should go ahead and I couldn't see anything. Suddenly the next step disappeared and I went flying. Over and over I rolled, down and down, until I landed on the basement floor on all four paws. Thank goodness for my yoga training.

My eyes did a strange thing then. They swelled in my face and beamed like flashlights. I could see in the dark! Piles of sawdust sat under the beams. Cobwebs swung from the ceiling. Spiders scurried. Against one wall on high shelves were watering cans, vegetable seeds, a rake, shovels and big cans of paint!

Then the crunching got louder. Termites! I sneaked up on one. I was so close, my eyelashes touched it. But I'd never caught one before. It was just about to leap away. So I ticked my eyes back and forth, left to right, right to left. It stood still as a statue. That's when I opened my mouth, slurped, and ran off upstairs. All the way, I chewed. I must admit it was a little crunchy, like pieces of rusty car, but it had a wild green taste like grasshopper.

I waited with a Cheshire grin for Francesca to go shopping. After she left, I bit the bottom of Tyler's jeans and yanked him down the basement stairs, pointing my tail at the paint.

"Amos! You found some paint! Newspaper and brushes too. But remember, I can't draw."

I had just hypnotized a termite. Maybe it'll work on Tyler. So I swung my tail up in the air back and forth, back and forth, purring slowly, "Purr-purr-pu-rrr-purrr."

Tyler's eyes ticked back and forth and glazed over. "Maybe I COULD paint a dog," he sighed. "Let's take everything out to the backyard."

Outside, Bruno was sound asleep in a brown heap. Tyler pried open the lids and set the paints in the sun on top of the back fence to warm them up. The labels read BENJAMIN MOON LATEX ECO-PAINT. SAFE FOR BABIES: WAVY GRAVY, MARTIAN GREEN, CHEESE YELLOW AND TOENAIL PINK. He spread out some paper beneath the bamboo.

I hopped onto the top of the fence and checked the paint. It was ready.

Just at that moment, there in the bamboo perched a fat bird. I sat very still and whacked my paw out. Wham! The bird flew up higher and I stretched to get it. My paw lifted up as my back paws flew in the air. Missed again! Next thing I knew, I was falling down...right on top of the cans of paint! All the cans heaved into the air and dropped down right on top of...Bruno! He lifted his head and howled. Only the whites of his eyes showed. He was staring straight at me and he was no longer brown but striped.

The next moment, he shot straight up and chased me into the street. Tyler burst out of the yard after us, running all the way down the block.

By the Chinese takeout, Mrs. Wang stood outside her restaurant waving a spatula at Bruno, who dripped paint on her sidewalk. His paws were so drenched in paint he kept slipping and sliding over the pavement.

In front of the junkyard, Motor Mouth roared, yanking at his chain and sailing high up into the air. His mouth looked like a big black cave. The junkyard workers stood behind the fence, pointing.

"Look, a dog with pink toenails!"

"A yellow face!"

"A Martian-green nose!"

"Bet he glows in the dark!"

Bruno paid no attention to them, chasing me for three blocks past the smelly dumpsters. Soon the Brute began to gain on me; he was so close I could smell dog food breath. Suddenly a door opened and I jumped in.

Inside, all kinds of machinery clanked and banged. I was in a factory. Big black belts cranked along. I leapt over them, and Bruno bounded right after me. Suddenly something soared in

the air and landed on my back, sticky and thick. I looked down. My left side was blueberry and my right side was cherry. Yuck! A pie! I ducked under a machine and out a side door into a dead-end alley. Tyler spotted me from the street and ran to me. I pointed my tail at the door of a building at the end of the alley and Tyler nodded. But when he opened it, Bruno came running out of the pie factory and dashed in after me before Tyler could stop him.

Inside, men and women were tapping on computers. Newspapers sat piled up everywhere. I jumped up on a desk out of Bruno's reach. A big guard grabbed Bruno's collar just as Tyler rushed in.

"I was painting a picture of a dog for your newspaper contest and..." Tyler gasped.

Everyone stopped typing and stared at us.

A woman in a suit stepped forward. "A brilliant idea, young man! Painting the dog itself! A gravy-green and yellow dog. And a blueberry and cherry cat as well!"

Everyone in the newspaper office clapped.

"The contest is not over until next week, but this will make a great story right now."

Flash! They snapped our picture for the newspaper and we walked out. Tyler held onto Bruno's collar tightly. As soon as we got home, he hosed the Brute down. But the colour didn't disappear. It just faded. Bruno was now tie-dyed yellow.

Back in the kitchen, I plopped down in Dead Cat pose and instantly fell asleep. I awoke to gentle stroking. Something was cleaning me. I opened my eyes. The squirrel's tongue had licked all the blueberry off and now was slurping up the cherry. I didn't say a word. Cats love to be squeaky clean. And we don't like water.

Afterward, the squirrel burped loudly in my ear. It smelled like blueberry cherry pie. It plopped down beside me and fell asleep, snoring as loudly as a dump truck. You'd think it had been exhausted by the chase too. That's a squirrel for you. All they think about is themselves.

ME:
HEROIC SLEEP

IT:
SQUIRREL
SELFISHNESS

chapter 10

Nutz!

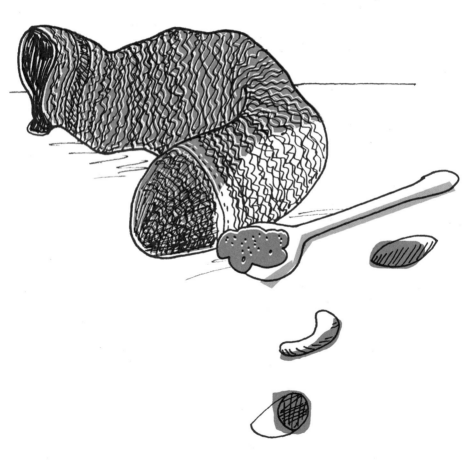

The next day began with another
chase, this time with a squirrel in the lead and a cat close behind. Francesca was off in dreamland, sound asleep. My catnip mouse had disappeared again. Take one guess who had hidden it. I chased that squirrel up the stairs, but it dropped Brazil nuts behind it as it scurried off. I skidded, plopped on my backside and went flying, landing in the sitting room with a thump.

"Give me back my mouse!" I meowed.

It replied with high-pitched staccato cackles.

Nuts were everywhere in the house: beneath the sofa, in the mop, in the flowerpots and even inside Tyler's sneakers. For a squirrel, keeping nuts hidden is like having a bank account. Rodents are always saving for tomorrow. I'm not that kind of animal. I like to spend, spend, spend and eat, eat, eat. I live for today. Who cares about tomorrow?

Late that afternoon, my life seemed about to change. The phone rang.

Francesca, looking very pale, hung up the phone.

"Mrs. Chu warned us that Stinky Feet is in the junkyard," she said to Tyler. "She went there to give Motor Mouth the bones. But the workers said he can't eat them anymore. And they probably told

Stinky Feet about the squirrel. We'll have to put the squirrel out right this minute."

"No way! It doesn't have a tail," Tyler protested.

"We can watch it in the tree with its family." Francesca petted the squirrel's belly. "At least you're not starting off hungry. You've got a potbelly just like Amos. I'll give you some pecans to go."

She slowly opened the back door. Outside, the bamboo waved in the wind. High up in the branches of the oak, we could see the old squirrel nest. The squirrel hesitated on the doorstep. It lifted its head, watching the darkening sky, the leaves blowing and the sun about to set. Then the Brute started howling and threatening death on everyone.

The little squirrel scampered back into the house, clicking its claws across the linoleum. It climbed into the sock and disappeared. The sock shivered and shook.

Tyler knelt down and spread his hand over the sock. "You must have bad memories of what happened out there. You have to stay here with us. We'll-find-a-way, won't-we-Mum?"

The sock grew still. One squirrel eye peeped out and gazed at Francesca.

"Alright...on one condition," she said. "You need to teach the squirrel to behave, follow house rules and go to the bathroom indoors. I was the one who trained Amos. Now it's your turn."

"No problem," Tyler said, smiling. "I can house train it."

"Muur-EOW!" That meant no in all languages.

"And we'll feed it something cheaper, like peanuts," Francesca said.

Tyler gasped. "Hey! I never thought about feeding it peanuts. We don't have any, but we do have peanut butter."

Peanut butter! The word was electric. The word was neon. The squirrel leapt out of the sock and ran to the cabinet ahead of Tyler. Tyler handed the creature a spoon smothered in peanut butter. The squirrel flipped the spoon around and around. It licked the peanut butter as if it were ice cream. Its eyes gleamed. As I watched the squirrel swallow the last drop of fresh ground Organic Easy Trade Munchy Peanut Butter, I knew it had licked its freedom away. It would never go back to the trees again. It was a keeper.

"Nutz!" Tyler shouted. "That's what we'll name it. It's nuts about nuts!"

Tyler and his Mum belly-laughed. Tyler even fell down and kicked his sneakers in the air.

But my heart sank in my furry chest.

SBA
SQUIRREL BANK ACCOUNT

WHO cares about tomorrow ???

IT LICKED ITS FREEDOM AWAY

"Nutz! Come on up here," Tyler said, sitting up. The squirrel flew to his shoulder like it had wings. "Now I can really train you. Bet you can do more things than just crack nuts."

Tyler had a new pet. He didn't need me anymore.

I went up to my room to be alone. I had a secret plan. I rubbed my cheeks over Tyler's blue jeans and kneaded my paws into them, smearing Amos scent everywhere. You could sniff me all the way to the Boulevard. Nobody would dare go near Tyler's jeans now.

No sooner did I finish the job than Nutz scampered in and sank into the pocket of Tyler's blue jeans like a pool ball. The nerve!

"M-E-O-W!" I shrieked like an alley cat. Then I whacked the pocket and Nutz went flying up into the air.

Tyler walked in. "Stop that, Amos! There is room for all of us in this house."

He must have noticed the nasty look in my eyes because he leaned over and lifted me onto his lap as he sat down on the bed. Then he petted my back until all my stripes lined up straight. We had a Tyler-Amos Talk.

"You know I love you, Amos. But I can love Nutz too. We are all brothers now. And you are such a big, sweet cat, I know you have room in your heart to love everyone too."

I let out a big sigh. Tyler's hands made me feel like a BFF again. When my back was stroked, I was mellow pie. Especially when he grabbed me underneath my chinny-chin-chin and tickled. Tyler thought he had sealed the deal. He even gave me the top of his head. I couldn't resist a Head Bonk and he knew it. I bonked back.

But what he wanted was impossible. I looked at Nutz and finally understood what bothered me. It wasn't his pointy teeth or the way he suddenly flew through the air without warning. The simple truth was this: he was a rodent. Cats eat rodents. You can swat a mouse flat with your paw like a tennis racket. But a squirrel will claw you. They're feisty. Ask my old pal Zach, down the alley. He's a tough ginger cat with four long scars on his head, scratched by a grey squirrel. Zach had learned the hard way.

Squirrels can't be house trained. That's because they are nuts!

Chapter 11

How to Toilet Train a Squirrel

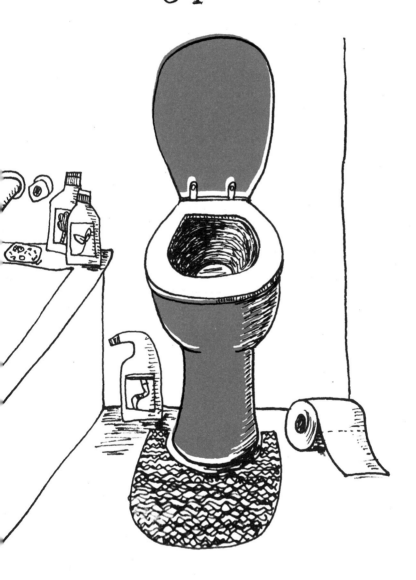

It's embarrassing but it has to be told. If it bothers you as much as it bothers me, then skip over this part. I won't mind.

I'm a no-sprinkle man. Francesca trained me that way.

Cat rule number 7: DO NOT SPRINKLE WHEN YOU TINKLE.

"You have better aim than any man or boy," Francesca once told me, proudly. "Not one drop on the toilet seat! You don't need a kitty litter box."

Lately, I'd been keeping post outside the bathroom. Tyler wouldn't be allowed to keep you-know-who unless he was toilet trained. Whenever I heard Tyler heading down the hall, I would rush in and sit down on the toilet. I didn't always need to go. I was just making sure the seat was occupied.

One day, I was perched on the toilet, really tinkling. The door was slightly ajar. I heard the squeak of sneakers in the hallway. Knock-Knock!

"Amos, can we come in?" It was Tyler.

I didn't say a word.

"Amos, remember how Francesca trained you to use the toilet and be neat?"

I did not budge.

"It's time for me to train Nutz. If he's going to stay with us, he has to be toilet trained."

The door swung open, and Tyler came in with you-know-who perched on his shoulder. Four eyes stared at me. I wanted to be alone. I was doing my business. I turned my head away so I wouldn't see them.

"Ah, the toilet is taken. How long will you be, Amos?"

I lifted my tail straight up and shook it like a rattle. This was a very serious sign. It meant I was in the middle of something.

But Tyler ignored me. He locked the door. This meant he was about to do something so top secret, he didn't want his mother to know about it.

"See that toilet, Nutz?" He pointed. "That is where you will do your business."

I watched as Tyler lifted Nutz off his shoulder and brought him right up to the toilet to see. When he flushed it, the squirrel shivered. I knew what Nutz was thinking. He was scared of all that water down there. I didn't care for it either. Nutz leapt out of Tyler's hand and ran across the floor.

"Come back here!" Tyler insisted. "You are going to do your business right now."

I had such a good seat, way up high, as I watched the rodent jogging in circles around the bathroom. He was very hyper. But I was very content because the toilet training was not going well. Instantly, I began a Full-Strength Motor Boat Purr. To do this, you must squeeze the back of your throat and all your muscles, even the ones in your chest and belly. Then the purr runs through you like a fast train. I didn't realize that my mellowness was contagious. The rodent yawned and stretched into Dead Squirrel. Tyler thanked me, lifted Nutz up, and set him on the edge of the bathtub.

"Look me in the eye," Tyler told the rodent. But Nutz couldn't; he was asleep. "Listen to all I say to you...Nut-zey...Nut-zey..."

Oh no. There's that falsetto again. Tyler was using his secret weapon. Nutz lay completely still. He barely breathed.

"Lis-ten-to-my-de-mand: You-will-now-pee!"

Tyler poked Nutz gently in the belly. His belly was very round and very full.

I couldn't let this happen. If the rodent got toilet trained, he'd stay forever. So I sprang off the toilet and hopped onto the edge of the tub too. My plan was to stuff my paws into Nutz's ears to block the hypnosis. But I was a little too eager. Or too heavy. I slammed right into the squirrel.

Nutz slipped right down into the tub. Our old house was on a slant. Everything in it ran downhill and so did the rodent, all the way across the tub, to come to a stop atop the tub drain. Nutz was wide awake now. And staring straight at Tyler.

Tyler lifted the eyedropper out of his pocket. "You've already drank about fifty of these. You must be full up."

At the sight of the dropper, Nutz began to do his business—right down the tub drain!

Tyler congratulated me. "Great thinking, Amos! It's a great spot for such a small animal!"

Nutz took another minute to finish. When he was done, he scampered back up to Tyler's shoulder.

Just then there was a knock at the bathroom door.

"Why is this door locked?" called Francesca. "Is Nutz done?"

Tyler unlocked the door. The two of them peered down the tub drain.

"What do you think?" Tyler asked. "Is Nutz neat?"

"Did he go down there?" She pointed to the drain. "I would never have thought of that."

Tyler nodded his head. "Sure did."

Tyler winked at me. Francesca leaned in and examined the drain. We all leaned in with her. I hated to admit it but the squirrel had a clean aim. The metal drain did not have one drop on it. It was as clean as the toilet seat.

Drat! That squirrel would never leave now.

"Perfect aim!" Francesca said, smiling. "He's drain trained now!"

"Good boy! Now Mum will let you stay with us forever."

Tyler fed the rodent a peanut. Nutz was in Nut Heaven. He gnawed away, scattering shells everywhere. He chattered to himself and Francesca and even me about how excited he was.

But Tyler wasn't done with the two of us. There was more training. He ordered us both into the kitchen and moved our bowls to separate corners. Francesca watched.

"These are the rules of the house," Tyler said. "Here's the deal. Lots of space makes good neighbours, so each of you has to eat at opposite ends of the kitchen. Amos gets the yellow bowl. Nutz gets the blue bowl. The squirrel gets my pocket. You get my bed, Amos."

Tyler and my mother waited for a sign. I could feel my eyebrows knitting themselves together. A pout was coming on.

"You still get my toes," Tyler coaxed me. "I won't allow Nutz near them."

I hesitated. It sounded a little better.

"If you seal the deal, Mum will boil you some gizzards right now," Tyler promised. "Nutz already got his peanuts for proper peeing."

Francesca looked at her watch. "It's almost time to go to work. Can you cook the gizzards, Tyler?"

"Yeah, sure. How do you do it?"

"Amos will talk you through the steps. He knows the routine. Well, Amos? Well, Nutz? Are we in agreement?"

Nutz shrugged his tiny shoulders and burped.

My head swung back and forth from Francesca to Tyler. Tyler stood in front of the refrigerator where a heaven of gizzards waited. This treat would be all mine if I gave in. What else could I do? I wound myself around Tyler's ankles and purred Full-Strength Motor Boat.

"Good boy!" Francesca petted my back. "We won't have to worry about Nutz living indoors now. But I am worried about Bruno. He looks terrible. Kind of gravy-coloured with a sickening yellow."

One of Tyler's ears twisted my way. I signalled back with two ears bent toward Francesca. She hadn't suspected a thing.

I waited at my post, first by the sink and then by the stove. What was so hard about boiling

gizzards? Just plop them in water and brew until the smell is so stinky, they're done. But Tyler got distracted. Up and down the stairs he ran, searching for his missing toothbrush. He's a fanatic about brushing before bed. Francesca trained him that way. He forgot to stir my treats or check if they had enough water. Two hours later, with no toothbrush in sight, my burnt gizzards were finally served.

Inside my mouth, the pieces were very hot, but no matter how much I chewed, the gizzards didn't melt. I couldn't swallow them. They tasted as bitter as rubber balls.

For the first time ever, I left most of the gizzards in my bowl. That's a record. I trudged wearily up the stairs to my bed. Tyler was sprawled out reading. I couldn't tell him he was a bad cook. After all, he was my BFF. When Francesca made gizzards, they were so soft they slid down my throat as if they were on skis. Maybe I should get Tyler a cookbook really soon.

There was a rodent in the tub, burnt gizzards in my belly and peanut shells everywhere. This house had been all mine before Nutz came here. It was a nuthouse. They could all have it to themselves.

I HAVE TO ADMIT IT: A CLEAR AIM!

WHAT'S SO HARD ABOUT BOILING GIZZARDS ?!?

TYLER NEEDS A COOKBOOK SOON!

Chapter 12

Runaway

I decided to run away, back to the streets where I was born. I had to get out of that house. Too many walnuts and almonds rolled around, tripping me up.

If you can't beat 'em, leave 'em.

After dinner that night, I squeezed out the front door past Francesca, who was putting out the garbage. As soon as my paws hit the pavement, I ran until my belly cramped up. All around me businesses were shut down for the night. Blackened windows of factories and warehouses stared at me. Nothing was the same as I remembered. In the distance, tomcats shrieked in a very high C. My nose twitched but did not tell me which way to go. I was lost. And all alone.

It grew darker.

I paused on the deserted sidewalk and listened. In the distance was a roar like wind rushing through tunnels. I crept ahead slowly. Around the corner stretched the Boulevard, like a monster blocking the way between me and my old home. Beneath my feet, the subway roared. In the distance, the lights of silver skyscrapers shone glittery and cold.

I couldn't cross the highway. I couldn't go back either.

I never told anybody what happened to my real family on the other side of the Boulevard. How my dad ran off to try Spanish food in Jalapeño Heights and never found his way back. How my mother, twin brother and I lived in the middle of a war zone where gang fights broke out every night between stray cats and dogs. And the final insult was that the restaurant owners didn't let us eat out of their garbage cans anymore.

"Homeless cats!" they yelled, throwing rocks at us. "Nasty creatures. Bad for business! Go away!"

My mother decided to cross the highway with us to live in Tyler's quiet neighbourhood. The last night I saw her, my mother had carried me across the highway in her mouth. I was six weeks old. When she went back to get my brother, I waited for hours as twelve-wheeler trucks rumbled past, but I never saw my family again.

Afterward I hid in alleyways in the new neighbourhood, where houses were ripped out like rotting teeth. Empty lots appeared. Repair shops, factories and warehouses were everywhere. Guard dogs barked day and night. Nothing to eat except flies and fleas.

Then Tyler found me hiding in the bamboo where a forest of leaves whispered in my ears.

He coaxed me out with stinky sardines. I allowed him to pet my back. His hands were as warm as cooked gizzards.

Tears rolled down my furry face. I'd never see Francesca again. Or eat gizzards. Tyler had saved my life. And I had left him. Were they looking out the window for me? Had they called the police? And was Francesca crying, just like me?

I turned away from the Boulevard to rush back home to them. The streets were a maze, winding everywhere. Every street was empty.

Until I rounded the next corner.

Two tomcats howled in the street right in front of me. They both turned their scruffy heads my way. One had lost an eye. The other one's face was marked with scars.

They arched their backs. They spread their claws wide. Catcalls vibrated through me like thunder and lightning. My paws took off. Up and down the blackened blocks the three of us ran, into the streets and over the sidewalks.

I shivered like I was a little kitten. My eyes shone like a searchlight, looking here, looking there. I gulped deep breaths, hoping to smell home: Tyler's soccer sneakers full of walnuts, the scent of Good to Go salami heroes, the odour of sliced onion and mayonnaise that clung to Francesca's hair and the hint of buttered popcorn on Tyler's fingers.

The two tomcats were silent as they ran. Their bodies were lean and swift. Behind me, they growled and closed in. That's when I ran into a big pile of pebbles and cement chips. Suddenly I was rolling over them. And then my brain cleared. I clawed the pebbles and shot them loose behind me, just like Nutz would do. I had learned something from that little guy after all. The first tomcat slammed into the pebbles head on and tripped. Next, I aimed hundreds of cement chips down the sidewalk. The other cat went flying and landed on top of the first cat. Both lay sprawled out on the pavement.

I sprang ahead, passing a building on the corner—the junkyard! Sudden barking filled the dark street, high-pitched barks nearby, and deep baritone barks from farther away.

Then I heard the voice: "Amos, is that you?"

Everything in the world slowed down. Tyler picked me up and squeezed me tight.

"Amos! We've been searching for you all night! I was afraid we'd lost you."

The tomcats sneaked off. The barks of Motor Mouth and the Brute faded. My Best Friend buried his face in my fur, and I purred in his ear—Full-Strength Motor Boat. I was back with my BFF, and no squirrel could take that away from me.

I was still purring when I got inside.

"Amos! You're back! I was ready to call the police." Big tears ran down Francesca's face.

Mrs. Chu was sitting beside her, patting her arm. "Poor Amos! Nutz has been quite a shock for you, hasn't he? No wonder you ran away."

Francesca petted my back. "Know what I'm going to do? Boil some gizzards for you. Just like old times. You make this ugly neighbourhood beautiful."

How warm the lights looked in the house. The chipped linoleum floor, cracked windows, even the ripped sofa, glowed. I spread out on Tyler's lap while Francesca made good on her promise to deliver the gizzards. The stinky aroma smelled delicious. My tail rose straight up and almost touched the ceiling. That's expectation for you! I'll bet even Cat Heaven doesn't have such fine treats.

Nutz jumped past, running out of the kitchen like it was on fire. His lips turned down. He began to sneeze. Maybe he was allergic. Then he headed upstairs to Tyler's pocket. I stretched out each and every paw, leaned my head back on Tyler's lap and waited.

"Come and get it, Amos!" Francesca sang.

My muscles quivered as I headed to my yellow bowl. While Francesca petted my back, I ate and ate, filling all the empty corners of my belly: the north side, the south side, the east side and the west side.

"We won't worry about your diet for a while, Amos," Francesca said.

"Good!" said Mrs. Chu. "Amos has been starving."

Nutz scampered back into the kitchen, looked at me and yawned. We both did a Downward Facing Dog stretch. Soon Nutz fell asleep by his food bowl. I hit the floor and sprawled out beside the squirrel.

"Just like brothers," Tyler said, smiling.

Yeah, right! Here's what my family did not know. Once I had gizzards in my tummy, I fell into a deep yogic trance. Even if the squirrel were shooting Brazil nuts at my head, I wouldn't care. No squirrel or boxer or even the hard peanut shells jammed between the floor and my back right now could bother me in such a mood. I was floating above them all. I was stretched out, stuffed and shameless, my big white belly facing up in Dead Cat pose. I was not my body. I was only my belly.

Om to Kitty Cats! Peace!

ALLEY MAFIA

chapter 13
The Party's Over

It'd been a month since Nutz had been rescued. And he was still here. There was every sign that he was a keeper. Yet the rodent had once lived outside in a nest high up in the oak tree. Bet if his family were still around, Nutz would join them and this house would be mine again. I began to plot.

The tree was in Bruno's territory and I was still a bit of a scaredy cat outside. All that day, Bruno's yellow nose was stuck in our fence and he cried big crocodile tears. Even in the rain, he was still out there pleading for bones. It had been raining for hours and I really didn't want to get wet, but I had to do this. I waited until the thunder and lightning stopped. The rain still came down, but it was lighter now.

At four o'clock, Bruno always went indoors for a half hour to watch the TV soap opera, As the Dog Barks. This was my chance. I headed out at three forty-five and waited by our house. Bruno lifted his nose straight up in the air and sniffed. Finally, the back door of our neighbour's house opened and Bruno ran inside. I must say his backside had got the worst of the paint. It was jungle green stripes with wavy gravy dots. I leapt onto the fence, tiptoeing along the edge until I reached the bamboo. A branch of the oak tree swung down near there. I jumped onto it, scurrying up to the old squirrel nest.

As I crept up to it, the branches grew thinner and thinner. They groaned and bent beneath my weight. Rain pelted down. But I pressed my paws down and slowly climbed ahead. Finally, I got close enough to peek into the nest. There was no sign of squirrel. Only broken twigs. I sniffed deeply. The scent had faded. No squirrel had lived there for ages. The nest was abandoned.

I felt something watching me. I looked across the yard at our house. Nutz was pressed flat to the upstairs window. The baby squirrel was completely still, staring at me. I stared back in the rain. He knew now—his family was gone forever, just like mine. We were both orphans.

Then the back door slammed. Bruno shot out like a sheriff on the hunt. I froze on the branch like a robber in a spotlight. The boxer ran under the tree and leapt up at me. I couldn't move. I couldn't even meow. At the window, Nutz ran in circles. Then he righted himself and pointed his paw to our yard. That woke me up. I dug my

ALSO AN ORPHAN!

BE FRIENDS?

mmmmmm...

claws deep into the tree, crept nearer to our yard, and jumped down.

Just at that moment, Tyler opened our back door. I rushed in and plopped down, breathless. Nutz scampered over. He ran his little nose up and down my wet fur, tickling me. Then he sat back on his haunches and stared. His eyes grew very dark and very round. He was admiring me like I was his big brother. Then Nutz did an odd thing. He leaned in close and his warm nose touched my cold nose. All around the world, in every neighbourhood of man or animal, that's code for "Let's Be Friends."

Before I had time to think about it, a strange odour drifted to our noses. Armpits. Garlic. Vintage 1889. An aroma brewing and fermenting on un-washed socks. I was the first to guess who was here.

"YE-O-W! YE-O-W! YE-O-W!"

Rain was pelting down and Stinky Feet was pounding on our front door. Nutz flew straight up and hit the ceiling. He fell back down and scram-bled across the floor, slipping and sliding at break-neck speed upstairs. Nutz could smell trouble.

"Let me in!" ordered Stinky Feet.

Uh-oh! The party's over!

All over the floor, walnut and peanut shells rolled. Francesca rushed around, gathering them up and throwing them into the cupboards.

"Tyler, answer the door. Stall him. I need time to clean up."

Tyler rushed off. We could hear him sweet-talking the landlord. Tyler's voice sounded like he had a cold. That's because he was pinching his nose. A stiff breeze of sweaty armpit blew through the house.

"Oh, so nice to see you, sir. It's been a long time. Where have you been? Great boots. Are they new?"

"Where is the rent, boy? And there'd better not be any truth to the rumours I hear about this house."

"Oh, no, sir, there are no rumours here."

"Boy, is there a rodent in this house?"

"What's the name again? A Mr. Ro Dent?" Tyler asked. "No one here by that name, sir."

Francesca straightened up. Her eyes turned dark as burnt toast.

"Amos," she whispered, "you have to help me clean up this place."

I looked around the kitchen. Evidence of a squirrel was everywhere. A supersized bag of peanuts. Walnut shells on the windowsill. Pecan pieces all over the table. So I did what Nutz would do. I grabbed the nuts between my teeth, ran off and hid them underneath the sofa.

Stinky Feet banged into the kitchen. I flew up the stairs, picking up Brazil nuts on the way. From the top of the stairs, I listened. Stinky Feet demanded the rent. Tyler spoke to him in the same calm tone he used with all animals. I could tell he was trying to put the landlord into a trance. I should know. Tyler had tried all those tricks on me before.

"You-might-want-to-sit-down-and-be-calm, sir," Tyler said.

Then there was another knock at the door and Tyler rushed to open it.

Stinky Feet's voice grew louder. He was climbing the stairs now. And Francesca was talking to him in staccato. Tyler rushed back into the kitchen.

"STOP, sir!" Tyler shouted. "Here's the rent we owe. I'll even give you next month's rent ahead of time. I won the newspaper contest! They just handed me a big cash prize for painting Bruno."

"About time you paid the rent! But I suspect there's a squirrel living here. I'm going upstairs to look right now."

His boots pounded up the steps. The whole house shook.

Upstairs there was every sign of a squirrel. In Tyler's bedroom, a trail of sunflower seeds on the floor led right to his blue jeans hanging on a hook. Nutz hid deep inside the pocket. Peanuts peeked out of it. Brazil nuts sprawled everywhere.

I waited in the hallway like a sphinx, my paws curled beneath my chest. Why should I budge? Once Stinky Feet discovered the squirrel, out the rodent would go, like I'd always wanted.

But something made me pause. I remembered how Nutz looked at me today when I discovered the empty nest. He had lost everything: his family, his home and his tail. Without that tail, Nutz would probably fall out of trees. I'd seen squirrels fan out their tails like parachutes to slow down as they flew great distances through the air. Then I thought about losing my whiskers. Without them, I could not have run in the dark that night the tomcats chased me. I would have bumped into things.

Poor Nutz. He'd be too slow to live in the wild. I hadn't been fair to that squirrel. Maybe he could be a brother after all. Perhaps I could even learn to hypnotize him someday. After all, it worked with termites.

So I scrambled into Tyler's bedroom, whacking the nuts beneath the bed, under the rug and into the closet. Then I dragged Tyler's sweatshirt and threw it on top of his jeans.

I whirled around just as Stinky Feet entered the room. He saw me and the one Brazil nut still rolling between us. I had to think fast. Tyler was wearing his soccer sneakers. I gave him the signal—Meow in Low E.

Translation: "Let's play soccer!"

Then I scurried across the floor and shot the nut over to Tyler's sneaker. My BFF is on the ball. Back he kicked it straight to my paw. Swoosh! That nut spun so fast, it was just a blur.

Francesca laughed. "Did I tell you we trained the cat to play soccer?"

Stinky Feet's eyes were bulging as he watched me. In the heat of the game, he moved closer to Tyler's jeans. Right beside his head, the jeans were moving. They were getting ready to walk all by themselves.

I had to distract him. So I grabbed the Brazil nut and slammed it as hard as I could. Smack!

Goal! Right between Stinky Feet's boots. He groaned. I rushed in to get the nut back.

"Go get 'em, Amos!" Tyler cheered.

Francesca clapped.

The landlord frowned at me like he was a fan of the opposing team.

All eyes were on me.

My head sank right between Stinky Feet's boots where the nut was stuck. A horrible odour filled my nose and went straight to my sinus passages. It was like I'd fallen into a barrel of garlic armpits. Cats despise a smell like that.

I did what I had to in order to survive: I fainted.

SURVIVAL
MOVE
FOR EMERGENCY
SITUATIONS

Chapter 14

It's a Deal

I awoke to cheering and sweet chirps.

"Amos, you saved the day!" Tyler announced. "Stinky Feet is gone and he never noticed Nutz. We won't be hearing from the landlord for a while. He thinks we live in a nuthouse with a cat playing soccer."

Nutz chirped a lively tune from on top of Tyler's shoulder.

Meanwhile, Francesca had phoned Mrs. Chu.

"Amos? Poor thing!" Mrs. Chu shouted in her soprano voice on her way in. She was wearing one pink sock. "What happened?"

"He got too close to Stinky Feet's feet, I'm afraid," cried Francesca.

"Amos has been exposed to the stink before," Mrs. Chu said. "I wonder why he fainted this time."

"What could the matter be, then?" Tyler begged. "Amos looks terrible."

I was lying on my back on the kitchen floor where they had carried me. Something felt like tickles all over my belly. It was very itchy. Mrs. Chu's hands explored my fur. She pulled my eyelids down to check the whites of my eyeballs, then stretched my ears wide and shone a flashlight into them. Next she took my temperature and yanked my whiskers. Then she poked my soft belly. Finally she shook her head, frowning.

"Gizzard withdrawal!" she announced. "Amos suffers from lack of gizzards, liver and other stinky innards. You still haven't been feeding him those treats?"

"Well. . . he got some last week," Francesca said.

"And I didn't cook them right," Tyler confessed.

Suddenly Mrs. Chu stopped petting my belly and screamed. She shone the flashlight on my fur.

"What's that? Something's hopping. Bugs! They're wearing shields and marching all over Amos' belly."

I gasped. Bugs on my belly? I looked down.

Flat brown bugs paraded on my fur. I'd seen them before in the bamboo. Of all the bugs in all the world, they were the only ones I've ever refused to eat.

Mrs. Chu plucked one of the bugs. Oh no! Don't do that please!

Too late. A familiar odour filled the air: garlic and armpits. We all pinched our noses.

"Phew! What are they?" screamed Mrs. Chu.

"Stinkbugs!" Tyler yelled. "They eat tomatoes and vegetables. But if they are bothered, they spray like a skunk. They smell nasty, like sour milk stirred up with snake poop."

"That's ridiculous!" Francesca said. "It's a stinky cheese and burnt rubber smell. Cheesy toes!"

"That's NOT what it is! It's rotten duck eggs!" Mrs. Chu insisted.

They were all wrong. Who's got the nose with super smell? Amos. And I say it's old armpits dipped in garlic. We all backed away. Mrs. Chu flung the bugs outside and scrubbed her hands.

"Where did they come from?" Francesca asked.

"Only one place...Stinky Feet," Tyler said. "They must have hitched a ride on Amos when he dove between Stinky Feet's boots."

"That's why the landlord smells so much, then," said Francesca. "Those stinkbugs probably hop onto his socks from the tomato plants and make a home inside his boots when he gardens."

And a Big Stink too. Phew!

"Should someone tell him?" Mrs. Chu asked.

"Someone should wash his socks. That'd be a big help," Tyler said, laughing.

Within the hour the smell of heavenly gizzards filled the kitchen and with one whiff, my stripes turned deep grey. Soon gizzards bulged in my mouth and slid down my throat. They were as soft as melted ice cream on a July day. All around me hands petted my back, smoothing my stripes until they lined up like a road map pointing straight to Cat Heaven.

Francesca smiled. "You're our hero, Amos! Gizzards every day for you from now on! Tyler told me how you helped him win the contest. Now we've paid the rent. What a clever cat you are for helping to paint Bruno. All this time, I thought he was sick."

"Such a lion of a cat!" Mrs. Chu said. "He must eat fresh gizzards from Huang's Market every day."

"You're the best friend ever, Amos!" Tyler hugged me.

I purred non-stop like a motorboat.

The phone rang. "Sssh! The principal is calling." Francesca hushed us.

"Oh, you want us to bring the squirrel to Show and Tell?" she said to him. "And you just saw the picture of the painted dog, Tyler and our cat in the newspaper? Sure, we'll bring Nutz and Amos to school. And Bruno too? But...what-a-bout-Tyler's-de-ten-tions? For-get-a-bout-them? Yes, sir!"

"Bravo!" Mrs. Chu said. "You're all famous!"

Tyler's cheering was so loud I bet it stopped rush hour traffic on the Boulevard that day. The

GIZZARD
WITHDRAWAL!

!! BUG ALARM !!

BONK!

two of us celebrated with so many Head Bonks, we got as dizzy as two Dancing Chicks.

Meanwhile, Francesca grabbed the mop and all the secrets of our house tumbled out: Francesca's gold earring, Tyler's toothbrush, thirty prize cat's eye marbles, leftover sushi, the queen and knight from Tyler's chess game, Mrs. Chu's other pink sock, my catnip mouse, even bones for Bruno.

Tyler whistled. "So that's where Nutz hides everything!"

It was time for a Cat Chat with Nutz. Good thing I was in a mellow Persian mood on my mother's side. Two hums were all it took. One sweet chirp from Nutz and I knew my catnip mouse would be safe on top of Tyler's bed. After all, didn't I go out on a tree limb for the rodent?

Mrs. Chu opened a window to air out the kitchen. You could hear the Brute howling loud and clear. Tyler flung a bone into the yard next door. Out of nowhere, in mid-air, Bruno leapt up and snapped it between his teeth. He wouldn't be bothering me for a while. So I wandered off and slipped out the back door by myself.

Sometimes you just have to get away from the house. Be in your own world. Think your own thoughts. Become someone new. When I get in a mood like that, I hide way back at the end of the yard in the bamboo. I'm not a bit afraid to leave the house anymore. I'd been around the neighbourhood lately. I love to stare at the bamboo stems dancing with a seesaw rhythm back and forth in the breeze. The hissing of their leaves is like a call from the jungle, back when cats were lions, when cats were kings. I feel anything can happen when the bamboo sings.

And so it had. I am Tyler's BFF. I've got Francesca wrapped around my food bowl. As for my little brother, the squirrel, let's just say we've made a deal.

For now.

The End

AMOS
KING
OF CATS !

AbOut the authOr and Illustrator

VIRGINIA FRANCES SCHWARTZ is a recipient of the Geoffrey Bilson, Silver Birch, MYRCA, Red Cedar and the IODE awards. Born in Stoney Creek, Ontario, she now lives in NYC where she is a full-time author.

Virginia really did have a squirrel in the house. And a big toilet-trained cat who was very jealous. And a boxer dog next door who captured the squirrel in the first place. And a brother who hypnotized chickens too.

She came from a family that rescued and loved animals. The neighbours often visited with cameras and tiptoed down the hallway to catch the cat in action on the toilet bowl, or to have a walnut cracked open by the squirrel. Virginia thought she was growing up in a nuthouse. And she was!

And, yes, there really are stinkbugs loose in the gardens of North America. If you see Stinky Feet, please tell him. But don't get too close! If I were you, I'd stay hidden in the bamboo with Amos.

CHRISTINA LEIST was born and raised in Germany. She now lives in Vancouver where she has been working as a graphic designer and illustrating children's books. This is the fourth book she has illustrated for Tradewind. Her books have been nominated for many awards, including the BC Book Prize, the Blue Spruce Award and the Chocolate Lily Award.